THE BATTLE IS JOINED

Stalker came up from his crouch, his face a shifting mass of revulsion, his fingers already forming into talons. The man stopped in his tracks and the woman screamed. Stalker swung his hand forward, opening the man up from crotch to sternum. The victim promptly showed what he was made of, his guts spilling out on the floor in front of him.

Stalker spun to face the screaming woman. "You think *you're* having a bad day?" he demanded. "Look at it from my point of view."

And at that moment Chuck Simon, with timing bordering on the supernatural, swung in through the smashed window. . . .

PSI-MAN

Stalker

Books in the PSI-MAN Series

PSI-MAN

STALKER

DAVID PETERS

DIAMOND BOOKS, NEW YORK

STALKER

A Diamond Book / published by arrangement
with the author

PRINTING HISTORY
Diamond edition / December 1991

ISBN: 1-55773-617-0

Diamond Books are published by The Berkley Publishing Group,
200 Madison Avenue, New York, New York 10016.
The name "DIAMOND" and its logo are trademarks
belonging to Charter Communications, Inc.

PRINTED IN THE UNITED STATES OF AMERICA

10 9 8 7 6 5 4 3 2 1

December 26, 2021

1

No.

"Rommel, come on . . ."

Forget it.

"I'm sorry you're annoyed, but there is no other way—"

Get neutered.

Chuck Simon flopped down onto a rickety folding chair that creaked under his weight and stared at the stubborn individual across the room. The room was barely illuminated by a flickering fluorescent bulb, the type that almost no one used anymore because of that annoying buzzing that accompanied it.

A smell of coffee and stale doughnuts hung in the room, and everywhere you looked there was luggage piled up high with various tags affixed to them in a dazzling array of colors. The floor was greasy and uncomfortable, littered with candy wrappers and old wads of gum, as if no one had come in and washed it for at least several years. This would have been an assumption not too far removed from the truth.

Also present in the uncomfortable room was a luggage

clerk, who was eyeing with a great deal of uneasiness the individual whom Chuck was addressing.

Chuck himself looked rather unassuming. He had just emerged from the men's room, after performing another of the casual changes of appearance that had become second nature to him by now. He was cleanshaven at the moment, revealing his square jaw line and rugged good looks. But his hair had taken on a distinctly blondish hue and was combed back, slick and flat. His blue eyes still sparkled with amusement, which was impressive considering that laughter did not come easily to him these days. He was wearing simple gray slacks, sneakers, and a zippered blue sweatshirt that covered a black T-shirt.

The individual he was having the argument with was naked.

Technically, that was. He was, in point of fact, having an argument with a dog. It was hard to think of the dog as "his" dog, because, although they were bonded in ways far more substantial than animal and master usually were, it was hard to think of this animal as belonging to anybody in the world other than itself.

The creature's name was Rommel, and he was the biggest damned German shepherd that anyone could remember seeing—and when you did see him, you would never forget him. His fur was light brown except for a large black spot on his back and, curiously, a "Z"-shaped mark on the fur of his forehead.

As if the fact that he was as big as a Buick weren't enough, he was also in psychic rapport with Chuck . . . not at all surprising when one considered what Chuck Simon was capable of.

Chuck himself wasn't considering that at the moment. All he was considering was how in hell he was going to manage to get on the train considering that the massive animal in front of him had made it clear that the accommodations were intolerable.

The luggage manager cleared his throat and said, nervously but firmly, "Look, mister, I got maybe another twenty minutes to get everything loaded on the train. What's the story with you, anyway?"

"It's under discussion," said Chuck.

"Yeah, well, it better be finished being discussed pretty damned soon," said the manager. "There's no way that Godzilla is going to be allowed on the train . . ."

"I know that," said Chuck tiredly.

"Unless he's a seeing eye dog or something."

Chuck was royally annoyed with himself. He'd pulled that exact stunt over the past several days—passing himself off as a blind man so that he could get the dog into a room with him at a luxury hotel here in San Francisco. But he hadn't been thinking about it when he'd obtained the ticket for the Bullet Train, and you had to identify yourself as handicapped at the time of purchase. He couldn't very well go back now and say, "Whoops, excuse me, forgot to tell you that I'm blind."

"I know that," said Chuck again.

"So Godzilla here is gonna haveta—"

"His name," Chuck turned in annoyance to the luggage manager, "is Rommel."

"Fine. Rommel here is gonna haveta ride with the luggage, in one of our special containers. Otherwise the two of you can't get aboard the train."

"Then how am I supposed to get to New York?" asked Chuck in exasperation.

The manager nodded toward Rommel. "Saddle up and ride him."

Chuck actually toyed with the mental image that suggested for a moment and then dismissed it. He turned back to Rommel and said, "It won't be uncomfortable. Really."

I don't want to be caged up.

"It wouldn't be like being caged up. Think of it as special private accommodations."

Fine. So I'll ride in your seat, and you take the special private accommodations.

"They wouldn't let me," said Chuck drily. "I'm a human."

Now you're going to blame me for your character flaws again?

"Look, can I ask something here?" asked the luggage manager, intrigued in spite of himself.

"Ask away," sighed Chuck.

The luggage manager shuffled forward slightly. He was an older man, in a permanent stoop from a lifetime of lugging luggage (which was probably why it was called luggage, Chuck figured, since you had to lug it everywhere), and he said, "You act like you're actually talking to him or something. Like you say stuff to him and he's really answering back to you."

There had been times before where Chuck would just try to brush off such observations, but he had long since learned that being straightforward was always the easiest approach. "Actually, I am," he said. "Talking to him, that is. And he answers me directly into my own mind, because the both of us are telepathic. Oh, and I'm also telekinetic, and on the run from a government organization that wants to turn me into a psychic assassin." He smiled ingenuously. "Anything else you want to know?"

"Nope," the manager shook his head. "Nope. That just about covers it."

"Good," said Chuck, going back to what he was doing. "Rommel, we have to get to New York."

Why?

"Because . . ." He cast a glance at the bemused luggage handler, who apparently had decided that Chuck was simply an overimaginative but rather harmless nut—harmless as long as he didn't turn the giant mastiff on you, which is why it paid to humor him. Chuck liked people who humored him. It was better than the people who tried to kill him. "Because things are too hot in San Francisco, Rommel. Because that government creep at the newspaper knows that we're here, and we've got to put some serious distance between ourselves and this city. With all the earthquakes and everything . . ."

"Oh yeah!" said the manager, shaking his head. "Terrible, terrible thing. Terrible what nature has in store for us, isn't it?"

Chuck's lips thinned and he did not reply. There was no need to bring up the fact that the earthquakes and natural disasters that had racked the Bay area the last couple of days had nothing to do with nature. That instead it had been the work of a berserk teenage boy who had been coming into a formidable elemental power of his own, and was making sure that the entire city was trembling in his grasp. He had intended to destroy all of San Francisco, and it had only been actions by Chuck that had prevented that calamity from taking place.

He shuddered every time he thought of himself, a Quaker, a proponent and lover of peace, firing round after round into the chest of the boy who he'd come to know as the Chaos Kid. It had killed Chuck to do it, but it had killed the Chaos Kid even more. He had literally felt damned if he did and damned if he didn't, but at least he was the only one who was now damned. Otherwise the entire city would have gone straight to hell, plummeting through massive cracks and crevices into the bowels of the earth. He'd saved millions of innocents, but at such a cost . . . such a cost . . .

He shook it off and said blandly, "Yeah, yeah. Terrible. Just terrible."

I'm hungry.

"You're always hungry, Rommel," he said. "I'm really tired of it. And I'm tired of you bucking me at every turn. You see that?" and he pointed at the extremely large cage that sat open nearby. "That is what you're riding in. And if you don't like it, then you can stay behind."

Why can't we just drive out of here?

"Because I gave the car to Carmen, Rommel. You know that."

The woman.

"Yes."

Nothing but trouble if you ask me.

"I didn't ask you. What I asked you was to get your tail into that cage, or, and I mean it, Rommel, you can and will stay behind."

You're bluffing.

"You think I'm bluffing? Try me."

The man and the dog glared at each other.

"Fine," said Chuck, getting to his feet. "Enjoy your life here in Frisco."

"Hey, wait a minute!" said the luggage man. "You're not leavin' him *here*, are you?"

"I wash my hands of him," said Chuck serenely. "He won't go. I can't make him. So he's on his own from now on."

"But . . . but . . . but . . ." said the luggage manager, looking from the dog to Chuck and back again. Chuck was already heading for the exit, and the manager turned to Rommel and said, with great urgency, "C'mon, doggie. Please? Into the cage? Huh? Please?"

Rommel gave a deep, annoyed growl in his throat, and then with barely concealed disdain, he padded over to the cage and got in. Chuck was alerted to this by the abrupt *clang* behind him as the overjoyed luggage manager slammed the door shut, taking care not to crunch Rommel's tail in the process.

You owe me, Rommel muttered.

"See?" said the luggage manager, patting the top of the cage. "No problem at all."

Chuck rolled his eyes.

He emerged into the middle of the terminal after being assured and reassured that the cage was going to be put onto the Bullet Train. The last thing he needed, after all that, was to discover that the dog had been left behind.

Suddenly Chuck came to a halt, aware that danger was imminent.

He reversed so that his back was flat against a nearby wall, and watched as various people came and went in the large terminal. Incongruously, the sound of Christmas music floated through the air, giving a holiday ambiance to a situation that was thick with menace.

They were watching the terminal. How could he have been such an idiot as to think that they wouldn't be? He had avoided using mass transportation all this time for that very reason. So now the one time he tried to avail himself of a little luxury, this was the result.

He couldn't lock on to who or how many or where they were, but he knew that they were looking for him. Was it the bum rummaging through trash in the garbage can? The woman who was standing impatiently with a newspaper and glancing constantly at the clock? The old man who seemed to be snoring on the bench?

Every person in the place now acquired an air of being

something that they weren't. It made him feel paranoid, but then again, it wasn't paranoia if people really were out to get you, and in Chuck's case people most definitely were.

At least, he told himself as he scanned the room, as least he wasn't in a situation where he had to be holding back Rommel. Usually when this kind of problem arose, he not only had to try and anticipate where an attack might originate, he also had to keep a mental leash on Rommel so that the huge German shepherd would not simply charge the enemy, teeth snapping and snarling all the way. Now all he had to do was deal with matters himself, and not get himself killed. Otherwise Rommel was going to wind up on the train in New York with no one to pick him up from baggage claim.

He stroked his smooth cheek and was relieved that he had, at least, changed his appearance again.

He was starting to get a feeling, an impression, and his gaze turned back toward the bum who was rummaging around. Then he saw it—the bum was wearing an extremely nice watch. It flashed just briefly from underneath his coat sleeve. And it was in very good condition.

He watched the bum very carefully. The bum slowly turned away from the garbage can and strolled in the direction of the benches. Then he sat down and seemed to be staring at the people who were hurrying in and out of the terminal.

It was a rather ornate interior, with high Roman pillars and rather cavernous ceilings. Whenever an announcement was made over the public address system, it tended to echo around to the point where you had trouble understanding what was being said. A large clock hung in the middle, and below it was suspended an arrivals and departures board listing the comings and goings of all the trains.

Chuck watched the bum closely.

Then he saw the bum very carefully lift his wrist watch up to his mouth and mutter into it.

Either the bum was hallucinating, and thought he was Dick Tracy, or perhaps he was indeed Dick Tracy. The whole expression of his face changed as he spoke, going from slack-jawed disinterest to intense concentration. His eyes also seemed focused on a particular point in the room, and Chuck now followed that gaze to see just who or what he was looking at.

It was definitely a who. A woman, dressed to the nines in a sharp business suit, with navy-blue blazer, charcoal-gray slacks, and a simple black necktie. She was trying to look casual, leaning against a pillar, with one loafered foot propped back against it, but she was holding a finger against her earring and nodding. Then she started to talk, her gaze wandering over the crowd, and it was the bum who was nodding and listening.

Beautiful. He had them pegged. He just prayed that they were the only two agents who were around at the moment. But between the two of them, from their vantage point, they were able to watch all the people who were heading down to their various gates through the series of archways that ringed the terminal. Which meant that Chuck was going to have one hell of a time reaching his destination.

He noticed the gaze of the bum slowly turning in his direction, and he quickly darted into the closest shelter before he could be spotted, which just happened to be the men's room.

And promptly landed himself in trouble once more.

Jerome Ryder had always thought that going to the men's room was not one of life's larger challenges.

When he walked in, there was a general faintly nauseating aroma that accompanied most public men's rooms, and from the practice that one usually gets while passing through life, he was able to regulate his breathing sufficiently so that it wasn't totally overwhelming or even totally obnoxious.

Ryder was a slim but muscular man, with curly brown hair that was thickly tinged with gray at the temples. He had thick eyebrows with wisps sticking upward that gave him a vaguely owlish look. He was casually dressed, except that now he was casually undressing, having closed the door of the stall behind him. With his pants around his ankles, he sat down on the toilet and proceeded to read his newspaper.

He had about ten seconds of peace, and then a low and nasty voice said, "Okay . . . hand your wallet out."

He slowly lowered his newspaper and saw a gun pointed under the door, aimed directly up at his stomach. It was a very old-style gun—Ryder hadn't seen the like in ages. Six cylinders, hammer—it was almost laughable by today's technology. It was, however, deadly in its own way, and could scramble his insides as effectively as the latest FSG 18.

On the one hand, he was glad that it wasn't aimed lower. On the other hand, the thought of dying of a belly wound on a toilet in the San Francisco train terminal didn't exactly make him feel any better.

"Now . . . now this is a fairly large mistake," said Ryder, trying to be calm. He tried to think about making a sudden grab for the gun, but any sudden movement would be easily detected. Nor could he attempt to kick the gun away. Under the best of circumstances that was a risky proposition. With his feet tangled up in his slacks, it was just flat-out unworkable.

"It'll be your mistake," came the voice, "if you don't do what I'm telling you to do."

It was the kind of low and strung-out voice that belonged

to a typical drug user. Perhaps the guy was a Snap addict, perhaps something else. Either way, it wasn't boding especially well.

Slowly he reached down into his pants pocket and removed his wallet. There was no money in it, of course, which is why carrying a wallet was so simple nowadays. All it contained was his Card, as well as some business cards and a photo of his fiancée. It was the Card that the Snapper was after, of course. The Cards were the be-all and end-all of financial life. The Cards were singular identification and monetary expenditure devices, extremely versatile, that were issued at birth and were buried with you at death. All financial transactions were done with the Cards, credited or debited to your personal account.

There was a nice little black market for such Cards, because faking them was dicey but stealing them was a snap. Snappers would frequently trade them in for a hit of their drug of choice.

Ryder tossed him the wallet. "Here," he said, his frustrated voice like iron. "Here. Just go, all right?"

"Promise you won't tell anyone I stole your Card, right?" came the voice whose owner he couldn't see on the other side.

"Right. I promise," said Ryder, seething.

There was a pause.

"Y'know, I don't believe you."

The hammer on the gun was suddenly drawn back, and Ryder broke into a cold sweat.

And then he heard the door of the men's room squeak open, and a surprised voice called out, "You okay?" The gun suddenly withdrew, and Ryder knew that he had seconds to get himself together and out of the stall to stop the punk, or otherwise some innocent fool with bad timing was going to die.

* * *

Chuck entered the men's room, glancing over his shoulder, and then suddenly got the impression that he was walking into even greater danger than he was leaving behind. His head snapped around, and his eyes widened in surprise.

Crouched in front of a stall, on his knees, was an unshaven man with dark reddish hair and faded, crummy jeans. A vest hung loosely over his matted chest. He had his arm stuck under the stall and, hunched over the way that he was, seemed as if he were vomiting or something—which, considering the general stench in the place, would have fit right in.

"You okay?" he asked.

In response, the unkempt man yanked his arm out from under the stall and aimed a gun directly at Chuck.

Chuck Simon took a step back in surprise, but his mind was already reaching out. In an instant he had snared the hammer of the gun, and when the gunman pulled the trigger, he was astounded to see the hammer fall so gently, so carefully, that it settled back into place with not enough force to disturb even a butterfly, much less a bullet.

He tried to fire again, but this time he couldn't even squeeze the trigger. This wasn't surprising, because Chuck was standing there, arms folded, mentally preventing it from being drawn back.

With an outraged roar, the gunman charged at Chuck, waving his arm and the gun while yowling at the top of his lungs.

Chuck sidestepped and caught the leading arm, which happened to be the one with the gun. He immobilized the arm, but the gunman kept on going, nearly wrenching the arm from its shoulder as he ran past.

Chuck turned with a quick pivot at the hips and slammed the gunman into a wall, smashing him against some crude graffiti. The impact caused him to drop the gun, and it clattered to the floor.

It was at that moment, while dismantling his opponent using some exceedingly simple aikido moves, that Chuck realized the gunman bore a passing resemblance to himself as he had appeared less than an hour before. Far more disheveled, perhaps, and certainly more wild-eyed and desperate. But the likeness was there, and in that likeness a sudden and incredibly devious little plan was born.

At that moment the stall door slammed outward, and a man with graying hair leaped out, frantically fastening his pants and looking around in confusion and anger. No doubt the intended victim of the would-be robber. It was a rather nasty little stunt the guy had pulled—there should be *some* functions in life one could still perform without being subjected to harassment and danger. Well, if Chuck pulled this off, the gunman wouldn't be harassing people for some time to come.

Chuck chose that moment to release his grip on the man. The scruffy individual yanked his arm free, stumbling to the floor and immediately scrambling to his feet.

"*You!*" roared the man from the toilet, and the would-be robber stumbled once before making it to the door and out into the terminal area.

The erstwhile-victim threw open the door, but now Chuck was right behind him. "Stop him! Stop that guy! He tried to rob me!" shouted the man, as the gunman darted toward the middle of the terminal, glancing behind him frantically.

At that moment Chuck clamped a strong hand firmly on the victim's shoulder and said softly, "Don't worry about it. He's going to get caught."

The scruffy man dashed toward the center of the terminal, and Chuck saw that the woman and the bum were watching the man intently. They were not about to blow their cover for some two-bit hood. But Chuck was about to make sure that he was more than that.

A real police officer now stepped into the man's path, reaching for his own weapon and shouting, "Hold it!" The man skidded to a halt and threw up his hands as if he hoped, in some way, to ward off the cop.

Chuck could not have asked for a more perfect gesture. From thirty feet away, he immediately reached out with his TK power and lifted the cop high in the air. There was a collective gasp of shock from everyone nearby, including the fleeing gunman—but nobody noticed that, for they were all watching the airborne peace officer. The cop sailed through the air as if he were on a string and landed with a thud on a bench on the far side of the terminal.

Someone else, a good Samaritan, was already in motion, charging the guy, and just as the guy turned in the direction of the new attacker, Chuck caused the Samaritan to rise up and spin like a top in place. Throughout the terminal could be heard the alarmed shout of "Whoa-oh-oh-oh!" from the human cyclone, before Chuck deposited him, dizzy and nauseated, to the ground.

Chuck mentally chided himself for such an underhanded stunt, but it was also going to be an effective one. The undercover people had seen more than enough. The woman yanked a gun from her purse and less than an instant later had it aimed at the scruffy man, shouting, "Freeze, Simon!"

The scruffy man spun in her direction, but, at that moment, the bum now had his gun out. It had a longer barrel, and he squeezed off two quick shots. They made a sort of whispered *phwtt* sound, and the scruffy man twisted in place, shuddering twice as the shots struck him in the back.

It had been exactly as Chuck had surmised. You didn't

stay on the run for as long as he had without getting a feeling for how your pursuers think, and how they would act in any given situation. The woman had served as a distraction, while the man was the actual follow-through.

The scruffy man sank to his knees, his head spinning as the drugs from the two tranq darts pumped through his body. There was no way that the government was going to kill someone as potentially useful as Chuck Simon—not unless there was absolutely no choice. Instead, they far preferred to do what they were now doing—rendering him unconscious and keeping him that way until they could get him to a safe facility. Probably a sealed room or something like that, with walls made out of unbreakable adamantium.

Sooner or later, of course, they would run fingerprints or retina scans on this guy and realize that he wasn't Chuck Simon. But the agents would swear that they saw him perform stunts that could only be done by someone wielding formidable TK power—someone like the man the government called Psi-Man. By the time they got everything sorted out, Chuck would be long gone.

The man who had been victimized was now running across the terminal, and Chuck lagged behind him, drawn by curiosity and an undeniable amusement at the zealousness with which the two undercover people were performing their activities. They were slapping electronic cuffs onto the wrists of the scruffy man, who was already snoring deeply, and the bum was saying with authority, "Keep back, everyone. We're undercover officers."

The hell they were. They were doubtlessly with the Complex, the government spy arm that was Chuck's most frequent pursuer. But they were hardly going to identify themselves as such.

Another man, dressed in a jogging suit, came over now and helped them finish applying the cuffs. Chuck let out a mental sigh of relief. So there *had* been a third one, one that Chuck had not noticed. Even if he had managed to take out the two he had spotted, the third one might have gotten him.

"This man tried to rob me! I want to press charges!" said the man whose ass Chuck had literally saved.

The woman stood up, dusting herself off. "This is government business. This man is a wanted fugitive."

"I still want to press charges—!"

"Listen, mister," the bum was now saying, "if it's your sense of justice you're concerned about, then don't be. This guy is a wanted murderer. He's going to be answering for that, and the penalties he'll be facing are going to be a hell of a lot stiffer than whatever he'd be getting for attempted robbery. Okay?"

The victim, knowing that that was the closest to satisfaction he was going to get, nodded wordlessly and stepped back as the agents hauled the senseless man to his feet.

The bum was frisking him and said to the others, "No ticket. Either he wasn't going anywhere or we caught him before he got one."

"Where's the dog?"

"Who cares. We'll find him later." The bum was clearly feeling his oats.

Chuck smiled mirthlessly. Stiff penalties, all right. Ironically, Chuck had killed in his life—dark, ugly splotches on his soul that he had trouble living with. Even though at the time he had had damned good reasons, it still didn't justify the action to him, and he was certain that he was going to burn in hell once this tortured existence of his came to an end. But ironically, those weren't the actions that the government was after him for. And the penalties they had in mind were rather unusual: They intended to lobotomize him and turn him into the perfect mindless, unquestioning assassin. They didn't mind if he killed, as long as he killed the right people.

They yanked the scruffy man to his feet and hauled him toward the exit, and several people actually burst into applause to see the forces of the law doing their jobs. The bum hung back long enough to flash ID to the clearly impressed police officer, who was still trying to recover from the unsettling feeling of being tossed through the air like a rag doll.

The man from the bathroom now turned to Chuck and stuck out a hand. "Ryder. Jerome Ryder," he said.

Chuck firmly shook his hand and said, "Simon Charles." He'd long gotten into the habit of giving some name other than his own, even to relatively innocent or innocuous people such as those he was facing now.

"You tackled that guy in the men's room, right?"

Chuck shrugged modestly. "It was nothing."

"It was a hell of something, all right," said Ryder. "Most people nowadays don't give a damn what happens to somebody else. And you were willing to risk your life over it. That takes one hell of a special person is what I say."

"Really, it's quite all right."

"Look, I'd love to buy you a drink, but I have to catch a train . . ."

"Yeah, so do I."

"At least let me—"

"No, it's okay. Really. Have a good life, and good luck to you," said Chuck gamely, and he turned and moved off. A certain amount of natural caution had developed, and he was reluctant to form any sort of friendship, no matter how casual, if it could be at all avoided. Everything in his life was transitory. That was the way things were for him, and he had come to accept it.

Nothing was forever.

2

BOB DARCY HAD been the foremost Bullet Train engineer for several years now, and he felt like he was stealing his salary. Studying the computer array before him in the control cab, he felt as if a child could run this thing. Or a chimp.

He tapped a series of pads, one after the other, as the on-board computer ran a series of redundant self-checks. He nodded approvingly. Absolutely everything was on-line and working perfectly.

The computer set and maintained speed, monitored all on-board power functions and systems, and generally was one hundred percent responsible for everything. It made Darcy, who was old enough to remember the days when an engineer really had some sort of function, nostalgic. The Bullet Train was one of the most desirable and highest-paying positions an engineer could get. You had to take all kinds of special courses and such to understand every facet of the operation. And then what happened? You got into the control cab and came face to face with the notion that the computer was more thoroughly versed in operations than you could possibly ever be, and was capable of processing information and activities thousands of times faster than you ever could.

He felt like a highly paid hood ornament.

There was an unexpected rap at the door, and he called out, "Yes?"

"Hello?" It was a female voice.

"Yes?" he said again, a bit impatient.

"Oh, is this occupied? I'll wait."

He blew impatient air through his lips. "This isn't a rest room, lady. This is the control cab." What the hell did the dumb broad think it was? You keep walking forward until you can't walk forward anymore, and you think that the front of the train was where a bathroom was located? Did people think at all anymore? Now granted, he did have his own private toilet facility here in the control cab, but he wasn't about to let some befuddled passenger make use of it.

"The control cab?" came the voice. "Is that like the cockpit?"

"Yeah, just like."

The voice turned sultry and alluring. "Ohhhh . . . I've always wanted to see that."

He cleared his throat. "I'm sorry, but rules are—"

"—Made to be broken," she finished for him. "I just consider cockpits such a turn-on. Don't you?"

He stared at the door for a long moment, and then swung around in his swivel chair and stared at the windscreen. Through the window he could see the beginning of the long stretch of track—the flat metal band that was the source of the magnetic force propelling the train. And in the window he saw his own reflection.

Not a young man. Getting on in years. Not going to have

all that many chances left for an unexpected rendezvous. So along comes some girl and . . .

"I really shouldn't."

"Please?"

God, she sounded attractive. He licked his lips and figured, What the hell. "Okay, but just for a minute," he said. He got up and walked the few feet across the cramped cab to the door. With a quick turn he unbolted it and opened it, praying that she had looks to match her voice.

She did. She was a big woman, close to six feet, with thick black hair and a bust that strained against a rainbow sweater. She wore a long skirt swirling around her muscular legs, and was carrying a large brown handbag. She smiled graciously. "You are soooo sweet," she said, patting him on his grizzled cheek.

"Yeah, well . . ." He shrugged, grinning like a school-boy idiot.

She sashayed into the cab and looked around eagerly. "This is incredible," she said breathlessly. "How does it work?"

"Well," he said gamely, closing and locking the door behind himself discreetly. "Much of it is computer . . . guided," which sounded better than "controlled." "I monitor all systems from here as the train rides on its cushion of magnetic force."

She turned toward him, leaning against the computer board. "I don't understand a lot of those technical terms," she said. "How fast does it go? The train, I mean?"

"We average 197 miles per hour," he said. "We'll be in New York in about 15 hours."

"Fifteen hours." She shook her head. "This is so marvelous for people like me, you know. People who want some sort of elegance. People who hate flying."

"If you want elegance, the Bullet Train is the ride of your

life," grinned the engineer. "Piano bar, holo-vid lounge, steam room, gym, private compartments—we call them parlors—you name it, we've got it. The new age of surface travel."

"It sounds marvelous."

"So," and he cleared his throat, "what do you think of our operation?"

She eyed him coquettishly. "I think," she said in a low, intense tone, "that you must get awfully lonely up here."

"It is, kinda," he said with a shrug.

"And I think," she continued, "that I wouldn't mind a little operation of our own."

His mind screamed *Thank you, God, I don't know why you're doing this, but thank you!*

She held out her hands to him and he stepped toward her, smiling like an idiot. He didn't care what he looked like. He didn't even care if she told him afterward that she was a pro and expected payment.

She took his head between her hands, and he said, "My name's Bob. What's yours?"

And suddenly the look in the woman's eyes shifted, or perhaps simply allowed something to show through that was invisible before. They were eyes that were twin black pools, and when she spoke again, it was with a dark, forbidding voice of a distinctly male timbre.

"Stalker," came the reply.

The hands worked with merciless efficiency, snapping Bob's head around so quickly that the engineer was dead before he could fully adjust to the fact that he was in any danger at all.

Stalker moved his hands apart, and Bob's body sank to the floor like a sack of wheat. Then Stalker unceremoniously shoved the body aside and sat down at the control chair, scanning the computer systems quickly and nodding in approval.

He punched a code into the computer board indicating to the central control system that the Bullet Train was ready to leave on schedule, which would be—he checked the chronometer quickly—in three minutes. Then he took the time to pick up Bob's body and stuff it into the small toilet booth that was to one side. That done, he then went back to the systems board to run a few last-minute checks.

Then he reached into his purse while whistling a tune that he was fairly certain was Mozart. He extracted a small plastic box, which he carefully set down, and from which he removed a small computer circuit board that he held up in the light gingerly by the sides.

It was the work of a few moments to dive under the control console and lay bare the inner workings. His fingers sought out the circuit board that he wanted, and he slid it loose with practiced ease. Then he inserted the one that he had brought along, dropped the original to the floor, closed up the console, and, continuing to whistle, ground the original circuit board to splinters beneath his heel.

He reached under his sweater and pulled out a bundle, his chest flattening down. Unwrapping the bundle, he laid out several large weapons, gleaming sharp and silver in the light of the cab. Then he took the clothes that he had wrapped the weapons in and, removing the dress quickly, changed into them.

The last thing he did was sit back down in the command chair and stare into the highly reflective windscreen that, only moments before, an aging engineer had been staring into, contemplating a decision that had proven to be fatal. The old man had made a mistake. Stalker did not pity him. Everyone made mistakes, and mistakes could be fatal. At least life was consistent that way.

Stalker reached up to his face, and he appeared to be concentrating. Then, like bubbling cheese atop a pizza, his face began to ooze, the skin running in rivulets over his skull, flowing into different parts and reshaping.

Engineer Bob, crammed into the toilet, didn't have anything to say in the matter.

Chuck heard the final "all aboard" call as he walked up to the Bullet Train. He stood there a moment, admiring it. He had to admit it was one hell of a piece of work.

It very much lived up to its name. It was large and wide enough to accommodate all the various luxuries that they had stuffed onto her. At the same time there was a sleekness and beauty of design that gave it the appearance of a bullet. A long red stripe ran the length of it, and the words BULLET TRAIN appeared on every other car. Along the tops, on either side, were thin iron bars that were used by maintenance crews to climb to the tops of the trains, where computer circuitry ran their length.

Through the soaked windows he could see the outlines of people relaxing in their small individual parlors—yet another perk of traveling on the Bullet Train. The entire vehicle had been created to be a nostalgic trip into a long ago method of travel. From what Chuck had heard, once upon a time, everyone traveled in such elegant, individual fashion.

Normally the Bullet Train was booked solid for months ahead of time. Curiously, the hideous calamity that had befallen San Francisco had opened up a number of reservations. Corpses made lousy passengers . . . at least the types of passengers who sat up.

He double-checked his ticket for the car that he was supposed to be boarding and stepped on. Once aboard, he was even more amazed by just how large the thing was inside. The aisles were wide enough for two people to pass side by side, as opposed to the way it was on buses or airplanes, where you had to sort of slide by to one side should you encounter anyone going in the opposite direction.

The individual first- and second-class compartments lined either side, and Chuck made his way down, glancing from one to the other and checking them against the number on his ticket. Everything was preregistered, although he had been assured by the ticketing agent that if he didn't like his assignment, he should come back and get reassigned. With all the craziness that had been going on lately, she had said, there was no guarantee that particular assignments might not get screwed up somehow.

He found the door with the designation K-13 on it and slid it open.

There was a woman already in there. She was quite a stunner. She had long red hair that cascaded around her shoulders like a burnished waterfall. A round chin, and pouty mouth, and large eyes . . . she looked familiar somehow. A question paused on her lips and she seemed to smile gamely. There was something else about her—she projected the impression of someone who had been crying a lot recently. Those large eyes were reddened and her shoulders were slightly stooped forward, as if she were carrying the weight of the world on them. And when she spoke there was a slight hitched sniffle tone to her voice.

The parlors were fairly large, with cushioned bench seats on either side that faced each other. All the parlors were built exactly the same, but in some instances you paid more for privacy and therefore had the designation of "First Class."

Chuck had done so, to avoid any more contact than was necessary. It didn't hurt him monetarily. The Card he employed was one of several that had been whipped up for him by wealthy and eccentric Wyatt Wonder, the movie producer and theme park mastermind whose life Chuck had saved. Chuck was never certain whether the charges he racked up on the Card were actually paid by Wonder or, more likely, somehow accrued into a never-land where the government was oblivious to its existence. Yes, probably the latter. Anything that he could do to scam the government was something that Wyatt Wonder would do without hesitation.

So to find someone in his first-class parlor was somewhat surprising to Chuck. Still, she was quite an attractive someone—it wasn't as if he'd been accidentally paired with, say, a trucker with a cigar sticking out of his mouth, or perhaps a crazed drug addict. Not only did she look harmless, but she was fairly easy on the eyes. Still . . .

"I'm sorry," said Chuck quickly. "I . . . uh . . . this is my cabin."

"It was supposed to be ours," was the reply. Her voice sounded vaguely Midwestern. And there was that deathly sadness in her tone.

"Ours?"

She looked down. "I'm sorry. I'll move," and she started to get up.

He put up a hand and said, "No . . . no, that's all right. Uhm . . . I don't mind if you don't."

"Really, I don't want to be a bother . . ."

"It's no bother." He smiled gamely. "I didn't know it was supposed to be ours. I had been under the impression that—"

"Not yours and mine." She looked down and was even more lovely when she did that. "I'm sorry. I must sound like a babbling idiot."

"Good looks forgive many social transgressions," he

said. "A harsh fact of life, but true nevertheless." He extended a hand. "Simon Charles."

She took it and shook it. She had a grip like a damp dishrag, as if afraid to let anyone firmly squeeze her hand. "Sandra Sendak. My friends call me Sandy."

"Mine call me Sy." *Psi*, he thought mirthlessly. He waved for her to sit down, which she did, and he sat opposite her after tossing his bag onto an overhead rack. On the rack opposite was her bag, an elaborate pink and gray number that was also a hanging bag. "Uhm . . . you'll pardon me for staring, but somehow you . . ."

"Seem familiar, I know." She seemed vaguely amused by it. "I'm a model. So you've probably seen my picture around."

"A model! That sounds like very interesting work."

She shrugged. "It has its moments. This year, women with nice asses are in." She stood abruptly and turned, presenting hers for inspection. The tight jeans she was wearing left little debate as to the quality of the ass in question. "What do you think?"

"Definitely of superior quality," he nodded gravely.

She smiled thinly and sat down. "Lyle always liked it."

"Lyle?" Now there was a name he had heard recently.

"Lyle Olivetti. Maybe you know him—?"

Why yes. He was the father of the kid who almost single-handedly destroyed San Franciso, not to mention California and possibly the entire world as we know it. "I know *of* him," he said cautiously. "You're a friend of his—?"

She laughed unpleasantly to herself.

A conductor came by, sticking his head into the parlor and asking to see tickets. Chuck and Sandy presented theirs, and the conductor glanced from one to the other. "Both of you have first-class designations," he said. "We have extra parlors . . ."

The two of them looked at each other, then Chuck said, almost as a question directed to her, "I'm okay here if you are—?"

She shrugged.

Part of him felt that this wasn't the smartest move he could possibly make. But it was such a bizarre coincidence that fate would bring the two of them together, and Chuck was a strong believer in the workings of fate. Except, of course, in those instances when fate conspired to make his life miserable. Then he simply believed in blind bad luck.

The conductor nodded briefly and then withdrew from the parlor.

"So, uhm . . . how did you know Lyle Olivetti?" he asked, trying to sound casual.

"We were lovers."

She sounded so matter-of-fact about it that it caught him slightly off guard. "Oh," was all he managed to get out, which sounded really intelligent. Which was followed by an equally pithy, "I see."

"I'm sorry. Did I shock you?" She put an additional, bemused emphasis on the last two words.

"No, no. I'm pretty tough to shock. I had heard that he was married, though."

She sighed deeply and settled back in her seat. She stared up at the ceiling and said wistfully, "He was going to be leaving her." Then she turned her level gaze on Chuck. "You don't believe me, do you."

"It's not for me to believe or disbelieve," he said evenly. "I mean, based on track records, married men don't generally leave their wives. Especially wealthy married men who have a lot to lose."

"He was going to. We were going to be making this trip

on the Bullet Train together. I've got a modeling gig on the East Coast, anyway, so it seemed like a good opportunity. Spend quality time together, he said. And then . . ."

Her voice trailed off.

"I heard," he said softly. "It was in all the papers."

She was silent for a long moment. "They still have no idea what caused it. That explosion that destroyed his house. Killed him. Killed his wife. Killed my dreams. No idea."

It was a bomb by a Soviet agent who was terrified that their son was going to destroy a lot more than that. Somehow that didn't seem to be the best response, even though it was the correct and accurate one. "I'm really sorry about it. It's odd, you know. To read about something in the paper, something about stuff happening to relative strangers, and then to actually meet someone whose life has been personally affected by it . . . it's just strange."

"Makes you think, doesn't it."

"Sure does." About what, he didn't know, but it made him think all right. He glanced out a window and said in surprise, "Hey, we're moving."

Sure enough, they were. The inside of the tunnel was rolling past them, and within moments they had passed out of the confines of the terminal and into the outdoors. As was usual, the sky was an overhanging, depressing gray. The color it had been yesterday, and the day before, and probably would continue to be tomorrow.

"This thing is smooth," she said. "Very . . . "

And then her lower lip began to tremble, and before Chuck knew what was happening, her entire body seemed to collapse and be racked with great, heaving sobs.

He went to her immediately, this total stranger, and wrapped his arms around her, comforting her. She simply sagged against him, soaking his shirt inside of minutes. He didn't say anything, but simply allowed her to let it out.

It was long minutes later when she finally composed himself enough to say, "I'm terribly sorry."

"It's quite all right."

"I have no right to be dumping all of this on you . . ."

"Really, it's fine. I don't have a problem with it."

He handed her a handkerchief, and she dabbed at her eyes with it. They were puffy and swollen, but still she looked damned good. "I don't know anything about you," she said, "and I'm using you as a crying towel."

"It just so happens that I'm a professional crying towel." He smiled. "So you see, you were lucky."

She smiled at that, and he chucked her under the chin.

There was the sound of boisterous laughter going past their parlor . . . several men, it sounded like, in the middle of some sort of celebration or other. What an intriguing place to have a party—on a train that was hurtling across the country at 200 miles per hour.

"I'm starved," he said suddenly, partially because he was, and partially because he was feeling a little awkward at the moment at such close quarters with a woman who was so emotionally vulnerable.

"Me, too, but I don't feel like going anywhere at the moment." She looked at him hopefully. "You think you could bring me back something?"

"I'd be happy to."

"Something vegetarian."

"Fine."

"I have to watch my figure."

"I'm sure when so many other men watch it, you have to keep your eye on it as well," he said with a smile.

She did not respond, but he hoped that she took it as a compliment. Then, without another word, he got up and headed off in the direction of the dining car to get some food for both of them.

At the moment that he stepped out into the hallway, however, an annoyed voice sounded in his head. *Are you quite through?*

"Rommel," said Chuck in a low, annoyed voice. "Were you listening?"

Of course I was listening. And it sounded disgusting, is what it was. Why do humans have to be emotional tangles?

"We aren't all as elegantly simple as dogs," he said, glancing around to make sure no one was passing by. The last thing he needed was for someone to come wandering past and see him addressing thin air.

Get over here. I'm hungry. And they haven't fed me.

"I was just heading over to—"

To feed yourself.

"Well, yeah."

Some friend.

"All right, all right," he said tiredly. "Hold on."

He went back into the parlor and shrugged in response to her curious look up at him. "Forgot something," he said, and pulled down the small case he always carried with him that contained the few clothes and valuables he had in the world. Then, to his annoyance, it slipped from his fingers and fell to the floor.

As he bent to get it, Sandy's eyes lighted on something and she pointed. "What's that?"

"Oh this?" He looked down. Around his neck, on a chain, he wore a spoon that had been bent into the stylized shape of an "A." It had been one of his first controlled exercises of his psi power—pretty mundane by the standards of what he had done since then, but this held a sentimental aspect to it. "I made it. First letter of my ex-wife's name."

"Think she carries a fork made into your first initial with her?"

He laughed. "Probably not." He walked out of the parlor with the bag stuck under his arm.

He quickly made his way to the far end of the train and the luggage car, where an annoyed Rommel gave him a desultory look from within the oversized cage. Chuck noticed with amusement that, according to labels that had been partially covered over, the previous occupant of the cage had been a gorilla.

Directly in front of Rommel was a small pile of dog food in a bowl, no doubt provided as a service by the train conductors. Rommel was regarding it disdainfully. He looked ready to swallow the entire dish.

Hope you're having a good time, Rommel said sourly.

"Stop complaining. Here you go," he said, and pulled a raw steak from within his bag. He would have had to feed it to Rommel soon anyway. Carrying unrefrigerated meat around with you wasn't the way to make friends and influence people. He tossed it to the great dog, who gobbled it up almost with one gulp.

Great. What else have you got?

Chuck sighed in exasperation. "What do you want me to do? Go out and slaughter a cow for you?"

Just bring it here. I'll do the rest.

"I'll keep that in mind."

He started to turn away and then Rommel said darkly, *There's someone on this train.*

Chuck turned back to him with raised eyebrow. "What do you mean? There's lots of someones on this train.

Someone wrong. Someone dangerous.

He frowned. "I don't sense anything."

Of course you don't. Humans have no sense of smell and

can't hear anything. So why should it surprise you that you don't notice this.

Chuck leaned against a trunk and stroked his chin. If there was one thing he had come to depend on, it was Rommel's highly developed sense of trouble, even more acute than Chuck's own. But it disturbed him that he was drawing such a total blank on this.

Let me out. Keep me with you. You'll need me on this.

That might be the answer. That Rommel was fabricating this, knowingly or unknowingly, in order to get sprung from his cage. Even as the idea occurred to him, he dismissed it. He didn't think that Rommel was capable of pulling such a stunt. Yet, now that the germ of the idea was there, he couldn't quite shake it.

"I'll keep my eyes open," he said.

You do that. And as Chuck turned away, the dog added, *Wide open.*

He then headed back up the train, moving quickly and efficiently from car to car. Yet now there was a certain unease to him, and he was constantly glancing around, studying every passenger or train employee who went past him.

He didn't sense anything. He found that doubly disturbing. Not only was something going on, but he wasn't getting any sort of sense of it. If his innate ability to sense trouble was deserting him, then it was just a matter of time, and sooner or later he was going to wind up either dead or a smiling hitman. Either way it wasn't a cheerful or pleasant consideration.

"Hey!"

He jumped slightly and spun, immediately and reflexively assuming a defensive aikido position.

The man who had hailed him stepped back, immediately respectful of the stance that Chuck had just assumed.

"Whoa! Hey!" he said, putting up his hands. "Slow down. No attack intended here, okay?"

Chuck recognized him immediately and mentally chided himself for his overzealousness. "Hi . . . Jerome, wasn't it?"

"Right, right!" said Ryder. He laughed and clapped Chuck on the shoulder. "First the man's my savior, then he's ready to take my head off!"

"Well, you know, you always have to be cautious," said Chuck, shrugging sheepishly.

Ryder draped an arm around Chuck and led him down the hall, chatting pleasantly. Chuck glanced out the smoked windows at the passing scenery and was amazed how quickly it was going by and how smoothly the train was moving. It was as if someone were moving the scenery on a high-speed belt and they were standing still, like an old movie effect.

"That looked like aikido just then," Ryder observed.

"Tomiki aikido," Chuck said, a bit surprised. It was unusual for the average guy off the street to recognize a particular style of fighting, particularly just from the defensive stance.

Ryder nodded in approval. "Ultimate form of self-defense. No offensive moves, just pure defense. Don't make a move unless that other guy attacks. That's the way it should be. Lot fewer wars would be started if that were the way of the world."

"That's for sure," agreed Chuck. Then, after a moment of thought, he said, "You talk like somebody who's been there."

Ryder regarded him with a raised eyebrow. "You're on target there, son. Talking to a former member of a top tactical team. Very hush hush," and he put a finger to his lips. "Can't talk about it. Not a word."

"Oh, okay," said Chuck.

"That's why I'm on this train, though," said Ryder. "Bunch of us are having a reunion. They disbanded us ten years ago, but, by God, they can't stop us from getting together now, can they."

"Guess not."

"Come on! They'd like you!"

"Well, look," said Chuck, feeling more uncomfortable by the moment. "Maybe it would be better if—"

"No, really! It'll be fine. The gang would love to meet a scrapper like you. Come on! My parlor's just ahead."

Chuck sighed, accepting the inevitable. Sandy Sendak was just going to have to wait a few more minutes, because the boisterous goodwill of Jerome Ryder was clearly more than Chuck was going to be able to handle.

He heard a good deal of raucous laughter from a parlor just up ahead, and it didn't surprise him at all when it turned out to be the compartment that Ryder stopped in front of. When old army buddies got together, it tended to be a little loud and raucous. He recognized one or two of the louder voices and realized that it was the rowdy bunch that had walked past his own parlor earlier. Maybe this wouldn't be so bad after all. If they were getting particularly noisy in his neck of the train later, then he could ask them to keep it down, and they might actually listen to him.

Ryder pulled the door open. It rolled into the wall noiselessly, and Ryder called out loudly, "So! You're not all here yet!"

The three men who were inside the parlor compartment shouted back raucous and even playfully acerbic responses, to which Ryder was grinning so widely that it was clear to Chuck he actually liked abuse being heaped on him from friends.

They were all older men, like Ryder. Two of them also

had graying hair, and one of them was bald with just a few silver fringes along the crown of his head.

"Boys!" he called out. "I want you to meet a guy who stopped me from getting a nice-sized hole put in me by some drug-crazed idiot. Simon, these boys are three of 'the gang of six,' as we used to call ourselves. They're—" and he pointed to each of them in succession. "Joe Arnoff. Frank Bamberger. Ike Stern. Where's Rita and Al?"

"They're getting settled into their compartment," said the one called Stern. He was the one who was the shortest, with almost no hair to speak of. He grinning lasciviously. "You know how it is with *married* people." The others chortled.

Turning to Chuck, Ryder said, "Rita and Al Karpen were both team members of our little group—"

"You didn't tell this guy about us!" said Arnoff. He spoke with a deep voice and, of all the men in the room, seemed to be the one who would most readily be designated as "the Stiff."

"Christ, Arn, give it a rest," said Bamberger, with a quick and ready smile. The slimmest man in the room, he had a light and unassuming air about it. "Nobody gives a shit anymore, okay? Jerry could broadcast it on the news and it wouldn't make a damned bit of difference."

"Well I didn't broadcast a thing, and Simon here is purely on a need-to-know basis. Satisfied, Arn?" said Ryder with good humor. Arnoff grunted, and Ryder continued, "Oh, and behind them somewhere is my fiancée, who can't stand any of my old war buddies but doesn't mind being along for the ride."

The way the men were standing, they were blocking Chuck's clear view to the seat on the opposite side, but now they parted so that Chuck could see the woman clearly.

She had thick brown hair, a face with features as delicate as a china cup, and a long neck that looked tremendously tempting to sink your lips into. She was dressed smartly and fashionably in a blue pants suit, which didn't draw attention to the fact that she had the most incredible pair of legs ever given to a woman in the history of humanity—they came up to about her ears, they were so long. She also had a heart-shaped birthmark on her left buttock.

This was not information readily available to most of the men in the room. Arnoff, Bamberger, and Stern didn't know it. Jerome Ryder did. So did Chuck Simon.

Their eyes met, and their mouths dropped simultaneously.

Ryder, oblivious of the reaction, said grandly, "I'd like you to meet my fiancée, Miss Brown—"

"Anna!" said Chuck.

"Charlie!" She looked like she was choking out the name.

The men were looking at the two people in confusion, and the most confused had to be Jerome Ryder. He looked from one of them to the other and said, "Uhm . . . you two know each other?"

"Only distantly," said Chuck.

"Yeah. Very distantly," affirmed Anna, her brown eyes wide with amazement. She looked at Jerome. "This is the man I told you about, Jerome. And I guess you two don't really know each other, though maybe you think you do. Charles Simon, this is Jerome Ryder, my future husband. Jerome Ryder, Charles Simon," and she paused wonderingly. "My former husband."

3

AL KARPEN STRETCHED and yawned, lying back on the seat that had been pulled out into a bed. Nearby his wife, Rita, looked down at him with arms folded.

"You're getting old and lazy, Al," she said, and slapped him on his belly. "You didn't used to get so tired so easily."

"Hey, so what?" he moaned in protest. He was rather jowly, having just dropped a goodly amount of weight at his wife's insistence. Exercise had managed to firm up the flab on his belly, but he hadn't been able to do a damned thing with the chin. "A man's entitled when he gets older to slow down a little."

"Why?"

"Because that's the rule."

"And who made the rule?"

"A man," he said good-naturedly. "Look, go on over to Jerry's parlor, tell him I'll be along in just a little while."

"Yes, I'll be sure to tell him you're trying to get some sleepy-bye," she said.

"Tell him whatever you want. See if I care. I just want to take a short nap, okay? A catnap."

"The cat doesn't nap as often as you do."

He smiled at the good-natured teasing and couldn't help but admire the woman. God, Rita had really held up. After everything they'd been through as a unit, to see a woman manage to look so damned good. He had a feeling her hair was graying, but she was so assiduous about her trips to the beauty parlor that it was hard to say. The rest of the face had maintained its shape—the high cheekbones and snapping eyes, the firm chin. Yes, a damned fine-looking woman. Sometimes he couldn't believe, in his heart of hearts, that she had chosen him.

She really did deserve his best effort.

He started to sit up, and then a massive yawn that bore a resemblance to a typhoon erupted from deep in his lungs. "Awww, honey . . ."

"All right!" she laughed. "All right." She waggled a finger. "But I'm coming back here in an hour, and you'd better be ready to go, or otherwise I'm going to drag you there, kicking and screaming."

"I'll be ready, I'll be ready."

"You'd better be."

He sighed inwardly. Rita was pathologically unable to let anyone other than herself have the last word. He decided to let it slide, or otherwise he was going to spend the entire hour arguing and not get a wink of sleep.

She slid out of the door, and Al settled back, his hands behind his head, his elbows pointed towards the ceiling. He started to feel himself drifting, sensitive to the slightest motion of the incredible train that was propelled on a cushion of magnetism.

There was a rap at the door.

"Oh, now what?" he called out.

"Conductor," came a voice.

"We already had our ticket checked!"

"Double check, sir. Apparently there was a forgery found. So we have to reconfirm all the tickets."

Blowing air impatiently out from his lips, Al hauled himself up and, scratching his belly, went to the door and opened it.

A conductor was standing there, smiling politely. And . . .

And immediately Al sensed something, his old warrior's instinct flashing at him as if he'd never stopped using it. The gang had always called him the Warhorse, and it was a name he'd lived up to. He'd also been called the Point Man, because it had always been Al Karpen who was the first one into any dangerous situation. He'd had an incredible knack for nosing out enemy traps, and that knack of his was serving him now.

He stared into the conductor's eyes. There was a hardness to them, and a cruelty, and a bitterness . . .

Without knowing or understanding why, but also without hesitating, Al Karpen tried to slam the door shut as quickly as it could. It rolled halfway shut before the conductor caught it, holding the handle in an iron grip.

The conductor stepped in quickly, his shoulder slamming into Al's chest and sending him falling back and onto the bed. Moving as if he had all the time in the world, the conductor stepped into the parlor and closed the door behind him.

"Who the hell are you?!" snapped Al, for he wasn't afraid yet. Concerned, angry, even furious, but not yet afraid.

"Don't you remember me, Point Man?" asked the conductor. "You Old Warhorse you? It's only been . . . what? Thirteen years? Lucky thirteen."

Al's mouth moved for a moment, and when he spoke, he was damned afraid. Because he *did* recognize the voice. It

was a voice that had haunted him for years, which still came
to him occasionally in his sleep and filled him with terror.
"St . . . Stalker?" he managed to get out, his voice barely
above a whisper.

The conductor nodded, spreading wide his hands. A
sardonic smile spread across his face. "The same. The very
same."

"They . . . they said you . . . my God . . . Stalker!"
All the blood had drained from his face. "They said you
were dead!"

Stalker came toward him, and suddenly there was a knife
in his hand.

Al scudded across the bed and opened his mouth to
scream, but Stalker was there too quickly. He clapped a
hand over Al's mouth, and he still had that same, lopsided
grin. And now there was an ugly and unpleasant laugh
resonating in his chest. The strength in the arm was
supernatural, keeping Al pinned against the bed despite all
the man's struggles.

Desperately, Al grabbed for Stalker's face, trying to
shove it away. It was exactly the wrong move, for Al's
fingers pressed against the cold and dead flesh, and horror
filled him. He tried to pull away, and the skin seemed to
elongate, to become malleable as melted putty. A long gob
of flesh remained attached to Al's hand and he screamed,
his eyes bulging out, his voice muffled by the pressure
against his mouth.

Stalker laughed. "Forgotten, Al? Understandable. It's
been thirteen years. Don't worry, though. I'm not going to
cut your throat. That's what you think, isn't it? That I'll cut
your throat?"

Al tried to nod in wordless terror, but he couldn't even
move his head. He whimpered, his eyes narrowing and
filling with tears.

Stalker jabbed his fingers down into a cluster of nerves at the base of Al's skull. The fingers were like steel rods, and Al felt his entire body go numb. But he was conscious, oh God, he was *conscious*, and the creature was still glaring down at him in that demented way that he had. That way that had plagued him for years and years . . .

He tried to stammer out some words, and Stalker brought an ear close to his mouth as if extremely concerned with what he had to say. "What was that? You're sorry, Al? That it?" Al tried to nod and couldn't so much as move his head.

Stalker slowly moved a finger along Al's face, tracing the line of Al's jawbone. "Now that's the problem, Al. I'm not sorry. Not at all. I'm just glad I was able to make this little . . . reunion. I'm going to be the life of the party."

Abruptly he stood, hauling Al upward as if the man had no weight at all. He dragged him into the small bathroom compartment, at the same time shoving his knife down into a holster on his forearm.

Al still couldn't move. If he could, he would have turned on Stalker and tried to destroy him with everything he had. At the moment, though, he had nothing. And he suspected that Stalker wasn't going to give him time to get anything else.

There was a sealed window in the bathroom, and Stalker drew back a fist and let fly. He smashed open the glass effortlessly, and immediately the bathroom was filled with the howling of wind rushing past at 200 miles per hour.

Stalker swung Al around and brought him up, face to face. "You remember what it was like to be born, Al?" he said in a harsh whisper. When Al only stared at him with wide-eyed terror, Stalker continued, "When your head came out first, and then your shoulders? You're going to relive that."

Al tried to get out the word *no*, tried to get out something.

Anything. A plea, a threat, a curse, something. But nothing would come, and then Stalker was shoving his head through the smashed window. The wind tore into his face, and now he finally managed to get a scream out, but no one could hear it as the wind whipped it away. His eyes narrowed to slits, the wind blasting away at his face, and he felt as if it were going to tear the flesh right off his skull and leave him a white-boned, grinning thing.

Stalker shoved him farther and farther out. First his shoulders emerged, and then he was dangling from the waist outward. The jagged glass from the window was digging into him, and thin streams of blood were trickling down his legs. The ground was barreling past at horrendous speed, a blur, and he prayed for something to happen, for something somehow to intervene and prevent him from tumbling out of the train to certain death.

He got part of his wish. Through narrowed eyes, he caught a glimpse of a large boulder, about ten feet high, situated on the side of the track. When he first saw it it was far away, and then within a breath—had he been able to take a breath—it was upon him. His mind barely had time to register the concept that the boulder was in his way, and then the thought was gone from his head . . . along with the rest of his head, not to mention everything from the waist up. It was left far behind as the trail hurtled forward, nothing but a reddish, pulpy smear all over the boulder.

Stalker smiled and released his hold on what remained of Al Karpen. A second later the force of the wind had sucked that out as well, and a second after that, the Bullet Train had left the last mortal pieces of Al Karpen far behind it.

Stalker stepped back out of the bathroom, shut the door and eliminated the rush of wind that had now significantly chilled and messed up the parlor. He looked around with an annoyed *tsk* and proceeded to straighten up. There was no sense in being untidy about this. No sense at all. And even as he did so, the skin of his features began to ooze and rearrange themselves once more, while he cheerfully whistled an incongruously happy little tune.

In the baggage claim area, Rommel's massive head lifted up abruptly as the dog awakened from his light dozing.

He sniffed the air, trying to figure out what it was that had roused him. But he couldn't detect anything—not physically at any rate.

Something was happening, though. Something was most definitely happening, and frustration overwhelmed him that he couldn't pin it down more. He wasn't sure where, and he wasn't sure how, but death was stalking the train, sure as anything. And he could figure no way in which to warn Chuck, because he wasn't sure what to warn him *of*. He had already voiced his reservations and concerns, but that was about all he could do. He hadn't been able to be more specific than he already had been, and without those lovely little specifics, Chuck seemed unable to function.

What worried Rommel further was that Chuck seemed oblivious to what was painfully evident to him. Was Chuck simply losing his ability to be psychically alerted to danger? Or, worse than that, was there something on board the train that was capable of masking its presence except on some primal level that Rommel was keyed into?

Rommel growled a warning low in his throat, as if the creature could hear him somehow. Yes, a creature, because whatever was aboard upon the train, there was much about it that made it other than human.

Stalker paused in his business, looking around, puzzled. Something had just brushed against his mind, something fierce. It didn't intimidate him. Nothing intimidated him.

But he was aware, in an offhand sort of manner, that something else was on the train that seemed to have a vague awareness of him. He filed that knowledge away, although it didn't seem as if it would matter all that much.

It did make him curious, though. His mental screens, part of his ability to fade into and out of any situation, should have completely hidden his presence to anyone—even a telepath. The ability to slip into and out of any situation was one of his greatest strengths—that, and the fact that he was a killing machine. Yet if something was aware that he was aboard the train, then that was going to make his little task all the more tricky.

Well . . . so much the better.

Stalker finished smoothing out the bed, then glanced over toward the main window of the parlor. In the dim reflection of the smoked glass, the face of Al Karpen smiled back.

4

"YOUR FORMER . . . HUSBAND?"

Jerome was looking from Anna to Chuck and back again. Then his gaze settled on Chuck for a long, confusing moment. His compatriots seemed to be a mixture of interested and embarrassed. "You told me your name was Simon Charles."

Mind racing, Chuck still kept a forced smile on his face. "Oh, I'm sorry. I'm sorry I wasn't clear. I thought it was clear. I'm sorry it wasn't."

"What the hell is he talking about?" said Arnoff wonderingly to the others.

Chuck wasn't sure but he gamely kept on going. "I was just introducing myself to you back in the station last name first, first name last, the way you had done. That's all. That's the problem with having two first names. Don't know why I did it. Just confused things. Sorry about that. Really sorry."

He was babbling. He sounded like an idiot, and felt pretty much the same way. But his mind had simply locked down on him. He had absolutely no idea what he was talking about, or what he was doing there, or where he was going. The world had dwindled away, everything becoming unimportant except for the fact that *she* was there, that Anna was there, and, my God, she looked so good and she still smelled so wonderful. And he was willing to bet that she still made those wonderful little cooing noises when she made love, remembering the way her hands would run the length of his body and . . .

"Well, this is a surprise," said Anna slowly, gamely, trying to act as composed as Chuck was clearly flustered. She seemed to be appraising him. "You're looking good, Charlie."

"You, too, Anna. Real good." Of course she looked good. She looked tremendous. She looked every bit as wonderful as he had remembered her to be.

The last time he'd seen her was in the office of her attorney, the guy he had colloquially referred to as "pond scum." This was back in his other life, the life before men filled with power and dementia had tried to kill him and the concept of just wishing someone would drop dead was an alien notion to Chuck. These days, he had been through enough to know that if every single agent of the Complex suffered a cerebral hemorrhage and keeled over, he wouldn't shed a tear over it and would, in fact, dance on their collective graves. But in the old days, those days that he had come to look upon as his relative innocence, Chuck had wanted nothing but good for all people and had believed in the fundamental goodness of every single human being. It was an attitude that he had since come to view as either simple naiveté or just out and out stupidity.

But the one man he would gladly have backed a truck over in those days was Anna's lawyer. He had come to blame that miserable little attorney for the divorce, because if he hadn't been there to make it so damned easy for Anna, she might have stayed with him and worked out the problems. She might have . . .

She was the only one who ever called him Charlie.

He shifted uncomfortably in place. "Real good," he said again, feeling like a tongue-tied idiot.

"Thank you. Your hair looks a little different. Different shade, I think."

"Yeah, well . . . changing with the times, y'know?"

She looked at him curiously, not quite sure what he was talking about, and at that point Ryder said, "So you're the guy that dumped Anna."

Chuck looked at him with astonishment. Ryder's face had hardened into thin, angry lines. "*I* dumped *her*?"

"That's what she told me."

He turned a surprised glance to her. "That's what you told him?"

She nodded helplessly, her hands moving in small, vague circles.

He didn't know what to make of any of this, or how to react, but he came to the sudden realization that he didn't care. He felt something just dead inside him, and he gave a mental shrug. "Okay. Okay, fine. Yeah, I'm the guy who dumped her."

"Charlie—"

"No!" said Chuck, his voice rising. "She's right. I just had my fun with her and tossed her aside like an old shoe. That's me. Love 'em and leave 'em, that's my motto."

"I will thank you," said Ryder hotly, "not to address my fiancée in that manner." The other three men were watching with the fascination of spectators at a tennis match.

"I shouldn't address her! I—" He waved it off, reining in his thoughts, which were blowing all over the place like snowflakes caught in a whirlpool of air. "Fine. Whatever you say."

"Charlie, Jerry, come on . . ." Anna began.

"Look, Chuck or Simon or Charles or whatever the hell your name is," and he took a step closer, his face now almost nose to nose with Chuck's. "You saved my ass back in San Francisco, and I'm not going to forget that. But you treated this little lady here like dirt, and I'm not going to forget that either."

"Jerry, please—"

He ignored her and continued tightly, "The way I see it, I should pop you one. Always swore that I would. But now I feel I owe you, so as far as I'm concerned, this squares it. In the future, you just stay the hell out of my way."

"Think he means it, squirrel," Bamberger said to Chuck in a laconic voice.

"Great. Fine," said Chuck. "If you'll remember, I was just minding my own business. You practically dragged me in here. So just don't drag me where I'm not going to be welcome, and everything should be fine. If you'll excuse me," and he pushed past the others and out the door.

As he did so, he practically knocked over a woman who was about to enter the parlor. "Hey, do you mind?" she asked. Chuck merely grunted a response and kept on going.

Jerome watched his receding form as the others welcomed and greeted Rita Karpen. Then he turned back to his compatriots and said, "Guys, I'm sorry you had to see that . . ."

"I'm not," said Stern cheerily. "A little soap opera livens up any gathering of old farts like this one."

"Speak for yourself, old fart!" laughed Rita, clapping him on the shoulder.

Ryder leaned over Anna and put a hand on her shoulder. "You all right, honey?" When she nodded slowly but didn't look at him, he continued, "You understand I owed the guy, right? So I couldn't have just let him have it, as much as I would have liked to. Just wouldn't have been right."

"No. No, I understand completely, sweetheart," she said slowly. "I would have done the same thing."

"But now all bets are off," continued Ryder. "That guy bothers you at all, or gives you any trouble, or even just looks at you funny . . . you come to me and I'll let him know what's what. You understand, sweetheart?"

She nodded, not really paying the least bit of attention to anything he was saying. It was all kind of fading out into a distant buzz, and one thing remained when all the mental static was cleared away.

Charles Simon, here, now.

Ohhhhh God . . .

Chuck stormed down the corridor, shoving past people and, uncharacteristically, not caring whether they were in his way or not. He ignored the muttered curses and the shouts of "Watch it!" Instead his entire focus was inward.

What was she doing here? Why now? Why her? Was it part of some divine plan; if so, then it seemed damn likely that that plan consisted simply of "Let's try to make Chuck Simon as miserable as humanly possible."

He shoved open the door of his parlor so violently that the wall rattled. Sandy Sendak jumped and gasped as Chuck stalked into the parlor, moving smoothly and with barely controlled anger. As the door rolled back shut, Chuck walked back and forth, stalking the parlor and trying to bring his fury under control.

Sandy watched him, marveling inwardly at the grace with which he moved, like a dancer or something. She couldn't help but notice that he'd brought absolutely nothing to eat back with him, but somehow now didn't seem the time to mention that.

"Problem?" she asked.

He turned toward her, seemed about to say something, changed his mind, walked a moment or two more, then turned to her again. "You're a woman," he said.

She looked down, as if double checking. "Yeeeesss," she said slowly. This promised to be one of her stranger conversations. She wasn't sure what the hell was going on, but, oddly enough, she welcomed it. Anything to get her mind off the great, empty space in her soul that had been created when she'd learned of the death of Lyle.

He dropped down into the seat opposite her. "Would you explain it to me?"

"It?"

"What women want?"

"I, uh . . ." She shrugged. "Happiness. Security. Success. The same things men want."

"No!" and he stabbed a finger at her. "Not what men want. Not what *I* wanted. And not only did she not want what I wanted, but she had the temerity—the *gall*—to lie about it to someone else!"

"She?"

He didn't even seem fully aware that Sandy was there. "All I ever wanted was a nice life. Quiet. Simple. But the small-town life wasn't good enough for her. Oh no. She wanted excitement. She wanted adventure. Oh, if she had only known . . ."

"Known what? And who's she?"

He put his hands up, palms facing each other, and stared in between them. "You have no idea," he said, "how often I've thought about her. How much I've been carrying a torch for her these past couple years. How often I've fantasized something just like this. That I'd run into her somewhere, somehow, and we'd be able to pick up where we left off. So what happens? I find her. I actually *find* her.

And she's hooked up with some other guy and lying through her teeth about me. How could she do that? How could she?"

Sandy shrugged helplessly. "I don't know how she could have. And I don't know what she did. And I don't know *who we're talking about*!"

He looked up at her in surprise, as if astounded that it wasn't obvious to her. "Anna!" he said.

"Anna?" She frowned. Then she caught a glimpse of the "A" dangling from the chain, and it was suddenly painfully clear. "Oh! Anna! *That* Anna!"

"Yeah. Right." He stood, hands jammed deep into his pockets. "That Anna. On this train. Here. Now. Today." He shook his head. "I can't believe it. I really can't."

"Weird coincidences happen," she said. " It's an old and trite saying, but it's also true: It's a small world."

"Well it just shrunk a few more miles today, that's for sure." He rubbed his temples, trying to shake off a headache. "I'm sorry to inflict all this on you. I mean, I don't even know you, and here I'm dumping the story of my life on you."

"It's no problem. Really. So . . . what? She left you because you were . . . ?"

"A teacher," he said. "A gym coach in LeQuier, Ohio. That was all I wanted to be was a teacher, and to live out my life there in that blessed small town. There's precious few places like it left in this country."

She nodded in quiet agreement. If there was one thing upon which everyone in America would agree, it was that the country was sliding downhill at an alarming rate. "It sounds wonderful."

"It was wonderful. And we met there, and fell in love there, and got married there . . ." He shrugged helplessly. "But she wasn't happy. She got bored, wanted to see the world. She tried to urge me to move to a big city. I tried to tell her that most of the big cities weren't places you'd want to even set foot in, much less live there. But she wouldn't believe me. She said that that was where the action was, and she didn't want to live out some boring, unfulfilling life stuck in the middle of nowhere."

"So she left."

"So she left," affirmed Chuck. "And she's been on my mind ever since. Every woman I see, I compare to her. Every relationship I contemplate, I think of it next to what I had with her and it pales."

"Other relationships pale next to a broken marriage?" She shook her head in wonder. "You're either a tremendous romantic or just thick, pardon my saying so."

"No need to pardon it. It's the truth. I've never been able to put that part of my life behind me. I've blown it up and idealized it to the point where she, and it, have attained some untouchable status in my grand view of the scheme of things. But no more!" he said firmly, slapping his hand on the seat for emphasis. "No more. Things are going to change, right now."

"That's the spirit," she said.

"I'm not going to dwell on her anymore. I'm not going to be intimidated by the thought of any woman but her. I'm not going to keep holding her in such esteem, putting her on some pedestal as the unattainable woman. You know what?" and his voice gained strength and confidence with every word, "I'm over her! Isn't that incredible? I mean, I didn't think it could happen so fast! I feel like a weight's been lifted off me, you know what I mean? I feel like, if I ever see her again, I can just laugh in her face and let her know exactly what she means to me, which is nothing! Nothing at all!"

"That's the spirit!" she said again.

There was a knock at the door and a woman's voice said, "Charlie?"

He grew pale.

"I thought I heard you in there. Can we talk, Charlie?"

He stepped back and hissed to Sandy, "Tell her I'm not here."

"*What*?"

"I'll go out the window and hang outside the train."

"What're you, *nuts*? You're going to break a window and hang outside a train moving at hundreds of miles an hour rather than talk to your ex-wife?"

He considered it a moment and then started toward the window.

"Charlie?" There was more knocking at the door.

Sandy grabbed him by the arm. "Now look, Simon, what happened to all that big talk a minute ago?"

"It was talk! Okay? I just . . . I . . . tell her I'm not here."

"No way, Cochese. I'm not getting in the middle of this. If you want to talk to her, you talk to her, and if you don't, you don't. But leave me the hell out of it."

She headed for the door and tossed it open. Anna was standing there, fidgeting uncomfortably with her pocketbook. The two women exchanged glances for a moment. Anna was clearly surprised by Sandy's rather stunning appearance, and she raised an inquisitive eyebrow.

Sandy turned toward Chuck with a mischievous smile and said, "He's all yours, sweetheart. I'm done." She blew a kiss in Chuck's direction and cooed, "Later, stud." And with that comment, she sashayed out the door.

Anna watched her go, and then turned her questioning gaze to Chuck. He shrugged helplessly and contemplated, one more time, the option of just hurling himself through the window.

"May I come in?" Anna asked.

He just stood there, and then finally shrugged and said, "I suppose. There's nothing stopping you."

She stepped in and slid the door behind her, then turned to face him. "You're looking good, Charlie."

"So I hear."

There was an awkward silence, and then she said, "Can I sit down?"

He gestured to the cushioned couch along the wall and she sat. He sensed her nervousness. Now why the devil was she nervous? She'd been the one who walked out on him. She was the one who had been in control of the relationship and then terminated it. What reason was there to assume that she shouldn't feel in control now.

Feeling constrained to say something, he said, "You're looking good, too."

"Really?" She smiled ruefully. "I put on a few pounds."

"You wear them well. Actually, you were a little too skinny when we were together." That was a lie. She'd been perfect. Everything about her had been perfect, and God, she was still perfect.

"You always knew just what to say, Charlie."

"Yeah. Obviously not just what to say in order to keep you with me."

She looked down, and immediately he regretted saying it . . . but at the same time, he didn't. There was so much of an impulse in him to hurt her, to lash out at her and give her some measure or taste of what she had put him through. Except he couldn't bring himself to do it.

"Won't your, uhm . . ." And he waved his hand vaguely. "Your fiancé be annoyed that you're here?"

"Jerome doesn't know. I told him I was hungry and getting something to eat."

"Jerome." He rolled the name over and placed a slightly

sarcastic edge to it. "So how did you hook up with *Jerome*?"

"We met in Oakland. I was working in a bank there and Jerome was one of my clients."

"You were a teller?" he said with amusement.

"I was an officer," she replied. "I have a business degree. You know that."

"Oh, I know that," he said evenly. "It's just that when you ditched me because you wanted to go off and experience the wild life of the big city, I didn't see you ending up as a bank officer. That's just so dry somehow."

"I didn't look for a 'wild life,' Charlie," she said, actually sounding a little amused. "I just wanted more than LeQuier had to offer."

"There were banks in LeQuier."

"But not the kind of life—"

"Dammit, Anna, *stop it*!" he said angrily, slamming his hand against a wall. "Just stop the damned lying and admit that you didn't leave LeQuier and you didn't want some exciting life. You left me, that's all. You were bored with me and you left me, and that's all there was to it!"

Surprisingly calm, she said, "Profanity, Charlie? From you? The Quaker with the heart as pure as the skies are gray?"

"Well, people change," he said tightly. He leaned against the window and watched the world speed past. "Sometimes people have to change, in order to survive."

"It wasn't you, Charlie. Why I left, that is. You're a good man. You were then and you still are. There was just something in me, that's all. There was something wrong with *me*. Not you. Something that just wasn't satisfied with my life, and so I had to go out and find a new one."

"One that didn't include me."

She sighed. "You're so determined to blame everything on yourself, aren't you."

"No," he said glibly. "I'm determined to blame it all on you, because you were too dense to realize what a great guy you had."

They stared at each other for a moment, and then she actually laughed. It was that soft, lyrical laugh, the one that had first attracted him to her. When he heard it, he couldn't help but smile, and laugh along because of its infectiousness.

"Now that's the kind of attitude I like to hear," she said.

"Why? Because it assuages your guilty conscience?"

She seemed to consider that. "Maybe a little," she said after a moment.

He was genuinely surprised to hear that. "What, you're saying now that you're sorry you left me?"

"Oh, I don't know what I'm saying," she admitted, and then seemed eager to turn the topic away from whatever it was running through her mind. "But what're you doing here, for heaven's sake? You acted like the world began and ended in LeQuier. Yet now here you are, on the Bullet Train, of all places. Going from one large city to another, crossing a continent. My Lord, Charlie, if I didn't see it with my own eyes, I wouldn't believe it. You never had any desire to travel, to see anyplace larger than the local mall. How did you wind up here, and with that extremely attractive young woman?"

"Oh, you mean Sandy?"

She glanced around slightly amused. "There's more than one in here? You're developing a harem?"

Evilly, he wanted to fabricate some long-standing relationship between himself and the stunning model. Just to watch Anna squirm a tiny bit. But he couldn't bring himself to do it. "She just happened to be here," he admitted. "Just luck of the draw. We never met each other before an hour or so ago."

"That's some considerable piece of luck. So what were you doing in San Francisco?"

He thanked his lucky stars that it was the holidays. School was closed for vacation anyway. It was odd—the high school he'd taught in seemed only a vague and distant memory. He had trouble believing that he'd ever been a teacher there. "With the Christmas break, I decided, you know, what the heck? I had money saved up. I'd never gone anywhere. And I figured, why should my ex-wife be the only one who gets to travel around."

"You had some timing, Charlie," she said, shaking her head. "That craziness that went on, with the weather and then the quakes. It was like the end of the world or something."

Damn near. "Well, that's me. Always showing up in the wrong place at the wrong time. Besides, you know . . . there's craziness everywhere."

"I like your spoon, by the way. What is it bent into, some kind of triangle?"

"It's an 'A'," he said gently. "For Anna."

She looked down., "Oh," she said softly, and there was silence for a long time afterward.

Rita Karpen and the others looked up as the door slid open and Al Karpen stepped in, smiling. "Al!" she said. "I thought you'd be out cold for ages yet."

He grinned gamely. "What? And pass up the chance to see all my friends? Nope. Couldn't put it off for another moment, no siree."

Arnoff, Bamberger, Stern, and Ryder greeted him with boisterous laughing and back-slapping and glad-handing. Ryder was the first to shake his hand, though, and when he did he blinked in surprise. "You feeling okay, Al?" he asked. "Your mitt's ice cold, man."

Al shrugged. "Ah, you know how it is. You get older, the circulation's not so good . . ."

"Rita, you gotta get this man's blood circulating," chortled Stern, and they laughed loudly, Al loudest of all.

Ryder draped his arms around his buddies and said, "I can't believe it. The SPEAR team, together again. After all this time. It's so great to see you guys."

"Yeah, well, you look like shit," said Bamberger.

"So speaks the expert," Al told him.

"Guys, guys, really . . . kidding aside. I'm so pleased you could all make this reunion," Ryder told them.

"But it's not just a reunion, is it?" Arnoff said quietly.

Ryder looked at him innocently. "What are you talking about, Arn?"

"Come on, Jerry," said Arnoff, stepping away from the group and eyeing Ryder skeptically. "This whole thing. I was in Chicago, Bamberger was in Detroit . . . we were all over the goddamned map. And out of the blue you contact each of us, offering to pay our way for this reunion, and this little excursion, ostensibly because of some big government bonus money added to your account. Come on! What do you take me for? What's really going on?"

"You know, you are the most suspicious son of a bitch on the face of the earth," Stern told him. Bamberger's head bobbed up and down in agreement.

But Ryder was smiling lopsidedly and shaking his head. "I can't pull anything over on you, can I."

"You mean he's right?" said Rita in surprise.

Ryder stepped away from them and leaned against the wall, so that he could address them all at once and watch all of their reactions. "I was contacted by the government," he said. "To be specific, by the organization that came in and basically made us obsolete."

"The Complex?" said Arnoff in surprise.

Ryder nodded eagerly. "They want to reactive the SPEAR team."

"Bullshit!" said Stern in amazement. "The government gave us our walking papers. Stuck us on a pension and told us we weren't needed anymore."

"Apparently they've changed their minds."

The others looked absolutely stunned—except for Al, who had a simple look of quiet amusement on his face.

"I don't get this," said Stern. "The Complex came in and became the umbrella organization for every clandestine and security group that the government worked with. And they phased out a number of the military-trained strike teams, including the Special Procedures Emergency Action and Reaction team."

"SPEAR," said Rita, "was told that it was outmoded."

"Well it seems we're coming back into style," said Ryder. "It appears there's things that the Complex is involved with that they're not making satisfactory progress with."

Stern's eyes narrowed. "What?"

"Now I'm reading between the lines here," said Ryder slowly, circling the room, "because you know these people. They only discuss things on a need-to-know basis. Volunteer nothing. But the way I'm reading the situation, the Complex is under pressure from people in the government— maybe as high as the President's right-hand man."

"Terwilliger?" said Arnoff. He spoke the name with a slight shudder.

"That's him."

"I met the guy once," said Rita. "Gave me the creeps."

"Same here," agreed Arnoff.

"We don't have to like him," said Ryder reasonably, "and he doesn't even really have to like us. What does matter is that he's getting impatient with the Complex."

"Impatient with them? About what?"

"Okay. Okay, look. There's rumors, see? Word out along all sorts of grapevines that I've been putting my ear to." He paused. "There's some weird shit going down these days."

"Tell me about it," said Bamberger. "The stuff in San Francisco—"

"That's just the tip of it," said Ryder. He drummed his fingers against the wall and said, "I've been researching this. Researching it for ten years now. Pieced together something from articles, documents, memos that were supposed to have vanished but never did."

"You were the best, Jerry," said Al. "When it came to gathering information, no one could top you."

"Thanks, Al. So . . . lemme tell you all a story."

"Oh goodie. A story," said Stern. "Can I have some milk and cookies with it, too?"

"Remember Stalker?"

There was dead silence. The various members of SPEAR shifted uncomfortably, having difficulty even making eye contact.

"Why bring him up now?" asked Al, with greater interest than any of the others.

"All right, listen. Once upon a time—decades ago—there was a disease that seemed to come almost from nowhere. It was transmitted sexually and a ton of people died from it. Remember it?" They nodded. "And then the government found a cure for it, and everyone was happy. The end. Except it wasn't the end. You see, that disease was introduced into the population by the government of the United States."

"Bullshit!" said Arnoff.

"I said it was a story, Arn," said Ryder calmly. "It's my story. I'll tell it, whether you like the way it's coming out or not. Now then . . . I didn't say that it was *deliberately* introduced into the population by the government. It might have been. It might not have been. To make you happy, let's say a sample accidentally got out of the lab, through the machinations of person or persons unknown. It got into the population. And the disease started killing people—but that's not what it was designed for. No, no. It was something that the government was only in the very early stages of developing. It was a virus designed to mutate those into whom it was introduced.

"The virus attempted to do its job. But in many people—far too many to even think about—their immune system tried to prevent it. Tried to drive it out of the body. So the virus simply destroyed their immune systems in its single-minded endeavor to accomplish what it had been designed to do. Unfortunately, killing the immune system meant killing the person as well, but go reason with a virus. And when they tried to find a cure for this virus, the virus simply mutated to avoid being cured. Why not? Mutations were its specialty.

"But in some people—in some fortunate people—the disease did not kill them. Instead it simply rested within them, not coming to its full deadly fruition. That's because what the disease was doing was changing them, just as planned. Their immune systems were fooled into leaving the virus, which quietly went on about its business. That business being to mutate the victims."

"Mutate them into what?" asked Frank Bamberger.

"Why, into superior beings, of course. Beings of specialized talents and abilities that the government could make use of. But with the mutational virus introduced into the general populace as it had been, there was no way to track it. Testing for its presence proved inadequate, especially because the people they really wanted—the people who were being affected in the way they wanted them affected—eluded detection. If the strain was doing its work quietly, tests didn't pick up its presence. Even more—and here was the most interesting aspect of it. If the virus didn't wind up destroying your immune system, then you wound up going in the other direction. You developed a bodily system so strong that practically nothing could make you ill."

"Except maybe this stupid theory of yours," said Arnoff. "I refuse to believe that the government was at all involved with any sort of freak mutation . . ."

And then his voice trailed off as he suddenly saw where Ryder was going with this. The others realized as well.

"Where do you think Stalker came from, Joe?" said Ryder quietly. "You knew that. You knew that he was part of a government project, since abandoned. The virus that became part of the general population could basically be regarded as phase one. Stalker was phase two—the first of a kind, and one of a kind. Then the crush of the Oil War fifteen years ago caused the government to press Stalker into action.

"Remember when the research lab that Stalker was created in was blown up by the United Arab Terrorist front? The men who created Stalker, the men who, in their youth, first developed the mutation virus that killed thousands, went up with that explosion. So did many of their assistants, not to mention most of their work. So there ended phase two—and phase three was an impossibility."

"That I knew about," said Al tonelessly.

"Other governments were trying their own mutations projects at this point. Since we'd just had our research blown to hell and gone, that's when the United States decided that the concept of eugenics was just too hideous to live. They didn't want to fall behind, so they figured that the easiest thing to do was stop everybody else."

"That's when the Eugenics War started, on top of the Oil War," said Stern, also understanding.

"All very hush hush, of course," said Ryder. "We'd gotten expert at covert operations, what with controlling all the news media. Mr. John Q. Public didn't know we were involved in one war, much less two. And that was just the way the government liked it. And that's when SPEAR was created—and Stalker was assigned to it."

"The germ warfare labs we blew up in the Ukraine . . ." said Rita slowly.

Ryder nodded. "Labs where mutations were being experimented with."

"Son of a bitch," said Bamberger, and Ryder could see that even Arnoff was accepting it.

And now Al spoke up. "Are you implying," he said, "that the Complex wants to reassemble SPEAR because they believe that Stalker is back in action?"

"Oh, no. No, of course not. Stalker's dead, Al. We saw him die. Nothing could have survived the explosion," said Ryder. "I'm amazed you'd even bring it up."

Al shrugged his shoulders and smiled gamely. "Just trying to allow for all options."

"No, here's what the story is with that," said Ryder. "You see, a few years back after the wars—after we took control of the Arab oil fields, and world governments signed a pact for no further experimenting in genetics—the Complex started a new program. They weren't experimenting in genetics, but they had something even better. There was an entire population out there filled with people who themselves had been, or had had parents who had been, exposed to the original mutating virus. The thought was that those people had the sort of abilities that the government could make use of."

"What kind of abilities?"

"Psionic, primarily. So they started doing tests throughout the country, all as part of some supposedly harmless government study into ESP. No one realized that what they were really trying to do was recruit people for the Complex to act as covert agents."

"Covert psionics," said Rita. She turned towards Al. "Do you believe this, hon?"

"Oh yes," said Al slowly. "You'd be amazed what I would believe."

"Imagine someone who could move things or start fires, just by power of will," said Ryder. "And if you think you can imagine such a thing, I can assure you that the uses that the Complex came up with putting them to was extremely impressive."

"How many did they find?"

"I don't know for sure," admitted Ryder. "As we move into more recent developments, the Complex has been far more efficient than the FBI or the CIA or MI or any of those outfits were in keeping their business to themselves. They are out there—that much is certain. How many and where is what the Complex has been trying to determine. But there's one name I did manage to find, as part of a misrouted communique in the Presidential office. Not a name so much as a code name. There's one guy who the Complex is apparently quite hot to get their hands on. He may very well be the reason that we're being brought together in New York. It seems he's on the run, and the government wants him bad. Real bad."

"What's the code name?" asked Al.

And Ryder said, "Psi-Man."

5

ADAM THALER, THE head conductor, portly and white haired, knocked impatiently on the door of the control cab and called out, "C'mon, Bob, what're you playing at? Open the door already."

Conductor trainee Rich Goldstein now came up behind his boss and mentor. Gangling and nervous, he pushed his glasses up on the bridge of his nose and said, "What's the problem, sir?"

"Ahh," Thaler made an impatient noise. "Routine status check, except for some reason," and he raised his voice slightly as he knocked more loudly on the door, "the engineer feels like making my life more difficult than it already is!"

"He won't answer the door?"

Thaler fixed Goldstein with an impatient glare. "No, he'd be happy to come out. It's just that I get such enjoyment out of standing here pounding like an imbecile that he lets me do it."

"Maybe he's sick or something. Maybe he's unconscious."

Thaler grimaced. He hated to admit it, but the kid had a legitimate point. Maybe he *was* unconscious. It had already occurred to Thaler, and when Goldstein voiced it as well, that was when Thaler nodded briskly and said, "Yeah. Yeah, maybe you're right."

He reached into his pocket and slid out a security card. He slid it through the receptacle on the latch, and the door immediately unlocked. Thaler pushed it open, Goldstein peering from behind him apprehensively.

It was the smell that hit them first. Goldstein wrinkled his nose up and said, "Cripes. Stinks in here. Like someone took a dump."

Thaler, however, immediately noticed the vacated console. The train was hurtling forward at 200 miles per hour, serenely under the control of the computer. The redundant human monitor was nowhere in sight.

But the source of the smell was readily apparent—the private bathroom just to the left.

"Close the door behind us," said Thaler quickly.

"Aw, sir, we'll be stuck in here with that smell—"

"I don't give a damn!" was the angry reply. He had a sick suspicion gnawing at him. "You want that stench working its way back to the passengers?" The first of the passenger seats were situated about thirty feet back of the command cab, separated off by a partition and a door that read, AUTHORIZED PERSONNEL ONLY. That was generally more than enough to keep nosy passengers to themselves.

Goldstein reluctantly but obediently closed the door.

Thaler, in the meantime, pulled on the door of the bathroom. It came open easily, for it hadn't been locked. And when Thaler saw the contents, he immediately understood why.

Bob Darcy was seated in the bathroom, stinking of the waste that had emptied out when his bowels released upon death. His eyes stared at nothing, his face frozen in a permanent expression of surprise.

Whoever had been capable of doing something like this didn't give a damn who knew if he was on the train or not.

Goldstein looked over his shoulder and started to wretch. He turned away, leaning against the wall, his insides heaving, but Thaler said sharply, "Don't you dare! Don't you dare get sick on my time!" The younger conductor looked at his senior in such surprise that it momentarily banished all thoughts of nausea from him.

"Wha . . . what do we do?" he asked in a voice filled with dread.

"We stop the train, that's what we do," said Thaler, crossing to the computer console. He paused only momentarily to kick the door to the bathroom shut with a backswipe of his foot. "We stop the train, tell the passengers that they should just bear with us while we get it sorted out. Then we contact the authorities, give them our location, and turn the cops loose on this. We don't handle it ourselves, and we sure as hell don't touch anything."

"Maybe . . . maybe whoever did this isn't on the train anymore," said Goldstein hopefully.

"Maybe. You want to take that chance?"

Goldstein wordlessly shook his head.

Thaler studied the console for a moment. "Okay," he said softly, "Okay, I remember how this goes." The console consisted of a variety of colored pads, all smooth and flat, all labeled, and all either glowing or not glowing depending upon what function was being carried out. Thaler's fingers ran across several of them, punching them in in rapid succession and entering the code that called for shutdown of the train's forward motion.

What would happen is that keying in the instructions would cause the great magnetic couplings of the Bullet

Train to reverse the polarity of the neutron flow, bringing the train to a gradual halt. With the velocity that they were moving, the last thing that they wanted to do was stop abruptly. The train might slam to a halt, but everyone and everything inside would continue to move at 200 miles per hour and wind up smeared all over the interior.

He entered in the correct command combination and waited for the computer to respond.

Nothing happened.

The speed held steady at 201 miles per hour, the world whizzing past in a blur. They were passing through flatlands now, the desert stretching around them in all directions, the gray sky hanging over them like an omnipresent reminder of death.

"What the hell—?" he muttered.

"What is it? What is it?" said Goldstein in concern.

"Computer isn't accepting the codes. Why would they have been changed? What would—" Then his eyes opened wide and he understood. "He did it."

"The engineer—?"

"Not the engineer, you damned fool!" snapped Thaler. "Him! Whoever killed the engineer! He did something to the computer! Reprogrammed it somehow, or maybe—"

"He changed a circuit board!" said Goldstein excitedly. "That's it. That must be what he did! So all we have to do is find out what he did and undo it and we can stop the train!"

Thaler was not remotely a computer expert, but nevertheless he gamely looked under the console to find the access panel into the guts of the command console. He located it in short order, but his heart sank and he spat out a curse.

"What? What?" said Goldstein, who was very much

starting to sound like he couldn't withstand much more bad news.

Unfortunately, that was all Thaler had to give him. "It's been sealed," he said. "Soldered or something. I can't get into it . . . not that I have the faintest idea of what I would have done had I been able to."

"We need help! We've got to tell somebody!" wailed Goldstein.

Thaler tried to ignore the panic that was rising in him as he stood again and tapped the panel that was a direct communications link to central headquarters. "Attention. Attention. HQ, Come in please. This is a Code 4 alert from Bullet Train Run Three Alpha Nine. We have a Code 4 emergency here. Please respond."

He waited for some sort of response but, at the same time, had a sinking feeling that his wait was going to prove futile. It turned out that he was correct, for there was no response from the headquarters in New York. Response should have been instantaneous, but instead there was just dead silence.

Thaler turned and looked at Goldstein, and didn't even have to say anything.

"Well . . . well this is good, then!" said Goldstein hopefully.

"How?" Thaler was willing to listen to anything.

"Because if communications are severed, then . . . then they'll know that something's wrong!" he said. "They'll try and intercept us. Or they'll simply cut the magnetic power at the source so that we're not powered on the track anymore!"

"Not gonna happen. Look." He tapped a light on the console that was labeled "Comlink." It was glowing serenely. "Whatever he did, he didn't simply cut the link. It's still open. The main function of the communications chan-

nel is to establish a steady voice contact with central headquarters. What he probably did was patch somewhere under
here," and he tapped the underside of the console, "a simple
voice message. We only have to check in once an hour. So
there's probably a recording sending through a message to
central HQ every hour that states our progress and that
everything is fine. And we can't access the communications
link to let them know everything is far from fine."

There was a long moment of silence, and then Goldstein
said nervously, "So . . . so what do we do? I mean . . .
what? We gotta tell somebody—"

Thaler turned on him so quickly that Goldstein jumped
back. "We tell *nobody*. Got that? Nobody. Because we
don't know what to tell them except that there may or may not
be a murdering maniac on board this train, and they may or
may not be in danger, and we may or may not be screwed
beyond all hope of recovery. Because for all we know this
train isn't going to be able to stop at all, and we're going to go
smashing into Madison Terminal in New York at 200 miles per
hour. Now you want to be the one to tell people that?"

"We . . . we could jump off the train—" Goldstein's
face was deathly white and the words were stumbling one
over the other. "We could just jump off and take our
chances—"

Thaler grabbed him by the front of his jacket and
practically bellowed into his face, "At *200* miles per *hour?*
What a great idea! Let's tell absolutely everyone that they
should just take headers off the train at 200 miles plus.
Leave a string of bodies dotting the landscape. That's just a
goddamn brilliant idea, you know that?"

"We have to do *something*!"

"Yeah. Yeah, here's what we do," said Thaler. "We tell
nobody else. We keep our mouths shut. We keep our eyes
open. And we pray that whatever's wandering around in the
train—whatever it is—that we see it before it spots us."

6

ROMMEL SHIFTED UNCOMFORTABLY in his cage, padding in a small circle to try and settle himself down. He wasn't succeeding tremendously.

There, in the back of his mind, there it was again. The uneasy feeling that something was terribly, terribly wrong. Something that he was sensing on only the the most primal of levels, but it was there, just the same. Something malevolent and deadly, and even though he couldn't pin it down any more than that, he nevertheless felt he had to do something. The tendrils of his mind reached out in the direction of the human with whom he had the closest bond on earth.

Al and Rita, wearing bathing suits and bathrobes over those, stepped up to the entrance to the steam room, nodding to another couple who was on their way out. They hung their robes on the hooks that were just outside the door, and then they stepped inside, closing the door behind them.

Rita took deep breaths, allowing the steam to soak in to

her pores and clear her sinuses. "Oh, God, this is great," she said. "I can't believe we're on a train."

"Neither can I," said Al distractedly. He was walking around the steam room slowly, almost as if he were checking it for traps or something. Some sort of inbred instinct. Then he turned toward her and smiled gamely, clearly putting aside whatever it was running through his head. He sat down and then patted the space on the small bench that was next to him. He also noted the bucket of cold water next to the door and the washcloths hanging over it, in case somebody wanted to dip in the towels and make a cold compress.

Rita came over, smiling, and sat down. She rested her head on his shoulder, and then the smile turned to a frown. "You know, you really do feel cold. Are you sick or something, hon?"

"Never felt better," he said. "Healthy as a horse. Besides, isn't that why you come to a steam room? To warm up?"

"Sure is." She paused. "What do you think of what Jerry was talking about? About reassembling SPEAR and all? Do we really want to go back to that, Al? I mean, aren't we getting kind of old for it?"

"I don't think you're ever too old for some things," said Al evenly. "Adventure knows no age barriers. In fact—how about a little adventure right now?"

She looked at him oddly. "What are you talking about?"

He smiled at her in a very strange fashion and then leaned over and kissed her. It felt very strange, because although his lips had warmed up to some degree, there was still a strange urgency about it that was far different from the almost casual way that Al approached her at other times. She returned the kiss tentatively, and then more firmly, for

Al virtually seemed to radiate an almost animal passion for her. It was refreshing, for truth to tell, the flames hadn't been burning quite as hot in recent days as she would have liked.

Then his hands were at the straps of her one-piece bathing suit, pushing them down. The steam and the mist and the incredible need that flowed from him all combined to give the entire thing an almost dreamlike feeling. She murmured only the slightest of protests, her heart racing, as the bathing suit descended to her waist. "Jeez . . . Al . . . somebody could come in any second," she whispered in his ear.

"That's the general idea," he said, a low laugh in his voice. His hands continued to work, and then she arched her hips slightly so that the suit was pulled down around her ankles and off.

She was trembling, every nerve ending of her body alive and tingling, and his face was over her in the mist, smiling down at her, his body atop hers, and she was covered with sweat, her breath coming in short gasps, and then there was a dripping on her face.

It didn't feel like water.

It didn't feel like anything she'd ever felt. It was thick and gooey somehow, and it was splattering onto her face—

Her eyes snapped open.

Al's facing was melting. His face and his entire upper torso were turning into rivers of oozing flesh. From within the hideous thing that had been his head, his eyes glimmered with cold amusement, and his teeth were pulled back in a hideous rictus of a smile.

Her mind screeched, bansheelike, within her head, a single name—*Stalker*.

"Al's dead. You're next," and his fingers dug into her throat.

* * *

Anna was just standing up and leaving when Chuck's head snapped around, his face suddenly becoming a mask of concentration. "Charlie—?"

"Shhh!" he said fiercely.

She stared at him in confusion as, within his head, a voice said, *Something's wrong. Something's really wrong.*

"What is it?" he said.

"I don't know!" said Anna. "What's what?"

There's a presence here. Something that wants to kill and kill. Something hungry.

The waves of concern flowing through his link with Rommel were too great to ignore, and Chuck became utterly oblivious to the confused woman who was standing a mere couple of feet away. "I don't sense anything," he said. "Are you sure?"

"Sure of what?" said Anna in frustration. "Charlie, you're scaring me. Is this some sort of joke or something, because if it is—"

"Shut up!" he said furiously. "Just shut up!"

She was shocked. Never in all their time together—even when she had told him she was leaving—had she ever seen his face twisted in such anger and impatience. And he wasn't even paying attention to her! It was as if he had suddenly found something a million miles away to be of more interest than her.

Yes, I'm sure. I'm the one with instinct, remember? We just keep you around for food and comedy relief.

"Can you lock it down?"

And suddenly the intensity of Rommel's sending increased, ringing so loudly inside Chuck's head that he thought he might lose his mind. *It's doing something! Right now! It's happening right now!*

"Where?! Where's it happening?! What's happening?!"

And Anna, completely confused, wailed, "Why are you asking me these things! Charlie, are you going crazy or something? Why are you—?"

And he grabbed her by the shoulders and said fiercely, "Shut the hell up! Anna, just get out of here! Just go!" He hurled her toward the door and spun away from her, looking off into thin air. Anna quickly slid aside the door and ran out into the hallway. She stumbled back, slamming into another passenger and knocking him on his ass. He let out a yelp, and she didn't even reply, because her heart was racing and she was utterly, utterly terrified.

The door was rolling shut again, but she could still see him inside, his hands outstretched like antennae, and he was saying, "Where? Where?" Then he paused. "Hot? What do you mean, hot? Someplace hot? Sweating, and—"

The door slid shut and then was immediately yanked open again by Chuck, his eyes wild. "The steam room! Something's happening in the steam room!"

The passenger whom Anna had knocked over, a big, burly man, was in the way, just getting back to his feet. Behind Chuck, Anna wailed, "Charlie, what's going on?!"

Chuck ignored her, starting to pull the burly man out of his way. Angered at being shoved around, the man stood his ground and said, "You little shit, are you the one who—?"

He didn't manage to get out a word past that, because Chuck knocked him flat without lifting a finger. He didn't know what was happening, but he sensed that nothing would be served by playing games with belligerent passengers. He lashed out with a TK bolt square into the man's chest, and for the second time inside of a minute the man fell backward, landing heavily on the floor.

Hearing the commotion, other passengers now stuck their heads out of their individual parlors to see what in hell was going on. Chuck paid them no mind at all, dashing past them, arms and heart pumping furiously.

Naked as she was, terrified as she was, shocked as she was, Rita's mind shifted into automatic pilot. When she had been with SPEAR, she had been the group's hand-to-hand expert. The fact that she was female, and a rather unassumingly short female at that, had served wonderfully on numerous occasions when the enemy had been caught completely flatfooted as she exploded in a cyclone of action.

She coiled her legs up, shoving her feet against the melting chest, and trying not to think about what she was feeling. Then the coiled legs unwound like a spring, muscles working smoothly under the tanned skin, and Stalker was thrown back, slamming against the wall.

She rolled off the bench, but when she tried to scramble to her feet, she was betrayed by the mist and sweat, and she fell to her knees, pain shooting through her legs. She gritted her teeth and started forward again.

And then Stalker was in front of her, shoving his right hand into the bucket of cold water. Then he yanked his hand out, dripping, and drew it back as if to deliver a karate chop. Rita braced herself, balanced on the balls of her feet, and Stalker's hand whipped around with the speed of a buzz saw.

She brought her forearm up to block the blow, prepared to deliver a counterstrike of her own.

Stalker's hand passed straight through her forearm. Her eyes widened in disbelief and sheer horror as her right arm plopped to the ground in front of her, leaving her a stump truncated at just above the elbow. Blood was already starting to fountain out, but she wasn't feeling pain yet because her mind had not yet accepted what it was that had just happened.

Stalker raised up his hand, which was now dripping with water and blood, and displayed it proudly. The edge had become razor sharp, like the blade of an ax. "Learned a few little tricks while I was being held captive," he said. "Not bad, huh?"

Rita tried to take a step to the right, tried not to think about anything except surviving and getting out, but she skidded on the blood pooling on the floor. Stalker's hand struck out again as Rita opened her mouth to summon a scream, and it severed her vocal cords. Blood streamed from her throat down her torso.

Stalker grabbed her hair firmly and drew her head back, ready to slice off her head entirely. The blade-hardness of his hand was softening up in the heat again, but there was still more than enough to do the job.

Her mouth was moving slightly, and he leaned close to her a moment, his face grinning and skeletal. Her lips puckered and then a glob of spit flew from them, smacking him in the face. This only prompted him to smile even more widely, a death's head smile.

And the sliding glass door of the steam room exploded inward, glass flying in all directions. A split instant after that, a blond-haired man leaped in and landed catlike only a couple feet away from Stalker.

Chuck Simon saw the mist billowing up from inside the steam room and, in faint outline, a male figure poised over a female, his hand drawn back and poised for some sort of blow that looked designed to be fatal. He could easily have just slid the door open by hand, but in his head the voice of Rommel was shouting, *He's there! He's there! I sense him!*, and spurred on, he simply formed his TK power into a spear and hurled it straight into the door. It shattered with a satisfyingly loud crash—hopefully enough to freeze the assailant in his tracks so that Chuck would have the moment he needed to save the life of the victim.

He vaulted through the door, watching his footing, and landed squarely, with a slight nudge of his TK power to keep him from sliding. He turned and faced the attacker, and his spirit and stomach recoiled.

It didn't look like a human being, but rather an undulating mass of reforming flesh. The woman was naked, and Chuck noticed to his horror that the woman's forearm was lying on the floor. The creature was standing in blood and didn't seem particularly perturbed by it. If anything, he reveled in it.

The creature smiled, teeth glistening through the oozing skin, and said, "Oh, are you in the wrong place at the wrong time! But first thing's first."

His hand reared back to strike the woman once more, and then it couldn't move. The creature's eyes widened in amazement, and now he pivoted back toward Chuck, his full attention on the blond newcomer.

"Are you doing this?" he demanded.

"Back away from her. *Now*," said Chuck, and for additional emphasis he mentally shoved the creature back against the wall. The creature smacked against it with a sickening *spluch* sound, and Chuck advanced on him, his gorge rising. Devoting part of his mind to keeping the creature immobile, he went straight to the woman and leaned over her.

Chuck touched her face, and it slumped over to one side, her eyes glazed over. The shock, the blood loss had been too much. She was dead.

He turned a furious and burning gaze on the creature and thundered, "What kind of creature *are* you?"

"I am," he hissed, his skin bubbling and seething across his body, "I am what I was made. And what are you?"

And for the first time, Chuck wanted to be more than what he was. "I'm the Psi-Man," he said. "And I'm going to send you back to hell, where you belong."

He mentally shoved the creature called Stalker so hard that he felt as if he could push the murdering bastard right through the damned wall. Then Chuck heard the commotion of voices approaching, and he glanced in their direction briefly, making sure not to let go of the monster he had pinned.

When he turned back to the creature, he was staring at himself. Except his face was a twisted, distorted, and evil thing. It was like looking into the dark side of himself, the monstrosity that he feared he'd become as a result of the violent and brutal life that he had had to live.

His mouth dropped in shock, and for just a second, so did his guard.

Stalker lunged forward, his incredible strength enabling him to momentarily break through Simon's TK stranglehold on him. He crashed into Chuck, broadsiding him, and Chuck tried to get a grip on him to hurl him aside. But his pliable skin oozed away under Chuck's grasp, making it impossible for Chuck to get any leverage.

Stalker turned quickly and slammed an elbow into the side of Chuck's head. The world spun around him momentarily and the Psi-Man went down, trying to recover, trying to center himself so that he could use his TK or his aikido, use some sort of defense against the monster. Then Stalker clasped his hands together and rabbit punched him. Chuck hit the floor, gasping, the steam making him dizzy, and he fought to maintain consciousness.

Stalker wanted to finish it, but he wisely held back. His skin had softened up in the steam, eliminating his ability to pull the razor fist again. And his opponent was still a powerful one. Chuck was stunned, but he could recover any second, perhaps even tear Stalker to shreds by pure thought.

Opting to get while the getting was good, Stalker started out the door, but there was someone there waiting for him. It was a young conductor, and for a split second, Richard Goldstein was as close to death as he had ever been.

But immediately Stalker saw the possibilities, and his hand clenched into a fist, lashing out and catching Goldstein squarely in the face. The lanky assistant conductor flew backward like a doll on strings and cracked his head smartly against the opposite wall. He sank down, moaning, his eyes closed, and Stalker leaped silently over him and bolted down the hallway.

Seconds later he was safely inside the parlor of the late Rita and Al Karpen, and breathed a sigh of relief.

Outside he heard a great deal of shouting now, and running feet, and screaming, and people barking orders to each other. More screams and yells of terror.

The Psi-Man. This was perfect. This was just too perfect.

Then there was a pounding at the parlor door. He froze, looking around and wondering where he could hide. Then he realized just how unnecessary that was—he still had the upper hand. The advantage was his. In fact, he had more than the advantage. He had it all.

"Yeah?" he grunted.

"Al!" came a frenzied shout. "It's me! It's Frank! Al, something horrible's happened! It—"

Stalker's hand hardened into a brutal, taloned claw, and he yanked the door open. Frank Bamberger was there, looking in the direction of where the chaos had been coming from, still bellowing "—It's Rita, something terrible, you've got to . . ." Then he turned back to face what he assumed to be Al Karpen, except it wasn't. Whatever it was

was shifting where it stood, skin being manipulated, eyes filled with hatred, transfixing the astounded Bamberger.

He grabbed Bamberger and yanked him into the parlor. "Excuse me, Frank, but it's time for a face-off."

As the door to the parlor rolled shut, the taloned hand lashed out and ripped off the front of Bamberger's face, as casually and quickly as if·scooping out ice cream. There wasn't time for a cry of fear or recognition or anything on the part of Frank Bamberger, or even a coherent last thought.

Stalker grinned once more, his face already starting to re-form into the image of Frank Bamberger. Then he picked the body up and headed to the bathroom, leaving a trail of blood and brains along the floor. It didn't particularly matter to him. He'd be taking over good old Frank's cabin now, which had to be in a lot better shape since it had not been the gory site of two murders.

And the Psi-Man, well, if everything went well, he'd be taking over a lot more than that.

Chuck staggered to his feet, his hands red with blood that had collected on the floor of the steam room, the soles of his shoes sticky with it. There was all kinds of shouting now in the hallway, confused babbling, and then someone screamed in terror. They were peering in and saw the bloody, mutilated body of a woman, and then others were looking in as well. One of them, Frank Bamberger, hurried off to meet his death, and then Chuck shouted, "Hurry! We've got to hurry! It's getting away!"

He stepped out into the hallway and tried to push people out of his way. People shrunk back and gagged as he left bloody handprints all over them, snapping impatiently, "Get out of the way! I've got to find it!"

He heard a voice cry out behind him, "That's him! I saw

him! That's the one who did it! He hit me, tried to knock me out! Stop him!"

Chuck's head snapped around to see a young and trembling conductor, with a bleeding nose and an eye that was already swelling up. "What're you talking ab—?" And he realized what the boy had seen—the creature with his face—but before he could open his mouth to explain, before he could fully focus his hazy thoughts, something crashed down on the back of his head. It was hard and metal—a fire extinguisher perhaps. Whatever it was, it was enough to send him to his knees.

"No! You don't understand! It's . . ." And then he was overwhelmed by the crush of bodies. He tried to shove them back mentally, but they were too many, and he didn't want to use lethal force against them. And before he could conceive some other plan, or even get out another comprehensible sentence, darkness overtook him.

Barking furiously, Rommel threw himself against the bars of his cage. The door creaked against his massive bulk, but held. He smashed against it again and again but wasn't able to make any significant headway.

You stupid human, he howled. *I warned you! I warned you!*

But there was no one to hear him.

7

CHUCK ROLLED OVER in bed and saw Anna smiling at him. She was watching him in that way she did whenever she woke up before him. Her head was propped up with one hand, her eyes sparkling in the morning sun. Outside the birds were singing, which was intriguing since the only place he'd ever seen singing birds was in the fairy-tale streets of Wonder World.

The tone of her voice didn't match the beatific expression on her face, however. She was saying, in a fierce, defensive tone. "He didn't do anything! This is crazy! Charlie would never hurt anyone, much less kill someone!"

Chuck now heard a voice from behind him, and he twisted around in bed. Jerome Ryder was standing there, hands on hips, and he was snapping, "The conductor saw him! He had Rita's blood all over him! Rita's dead, Al's missing, this guy is found on the scene with Rita's blood on his hands, and he punches out the conductor just to add to things. How much more proof do you want? Goddammit, Anna, we should just ice the little shit right now!"

"Don't you dare! Don't you dare, Jerry, or so help me

God, I'll walk out on you when we get to New York and I'll never speak to you again."

None of this was making any sense. Nor did he understand why his shoulders suddenly were aching, or why he could not move his hands.

Then he realized—they were tied behind his back.

He shook his head to try and clear the fog, and now the world went from his bedroom to absolute blackness. But there was a more tangible blackness, and the pain in his back came into sharper relief.

Finally he understood in a deep, throbbingly aching kind of way. He was blindfolded, and his hands were tied behind his back. He moaned softly and said, "Excuse me . . ."

"Shut up, you dumb little shit!" snapped the voice of Jerome Ryder.

"Don't call him that!" That was Anna.

"Yeah," said Chuck raggedly. "Who're you calling little?"

The direction of Ryder's voice changed, to come from directly in front of him. "You seem to think this is funny."

"No," replied Chuck sharply. "I think this is crazy. I mean, some lunatic creature from the pits of hell is out there cutting women to shreds, and you've got me hog-tied."

There was another voice, one of the men whom Chuck had met earlier. "We've got hog-tied exactly who we want hog-tied. The hog who murdered our friend!" And suddenly there was a quick rush of air that warned Chuck barely in time. A sharp kick landed in his ribs and he rode with it. He rolled and came up to his knees.

"Stop it!" came Anna's voice. "Stop it, Joe! Leave him the hell alone!"

Ignoring her, Joe drew back his leg to kick him again. "Jerry, make him stop!" she cried out, but it was clear to Chuck that Jerry was going to do no such thing. However, it didn't matter, because Chuck had a sense of where good old Joe was standing. He twisted his torso around, and the kick whistled past him. Knowing that good old Joe would be momentarily off balance, Chuck lashed out with one leg which, apparently, Jerry and his buddies had not seen fit to tie up. He hooked the tip of his foot around the inside of Joe's knee and pulled back. The rapid move overbalanced Joe, his knee buckling under him, and he fell heavily to the ground.

There was sudden shouting within the room, and Chuck, still angry over his shabby treatment, lunged forward and landed with both knees on Joe's rib cage. It knocked the breath out of him and caused even more shouting from the others.

"Shut up!" Jerry was yelling, and now cold hands closed around Chuck's back and pulled him off of the gasping Joe. "Just shut up, all of you. Simon—you're under the arrest of the United States government!"

Chuck felt a cold chill go through him. "The government?" he said, trying to keep the alarm out of his voice. "Really? Is it against the law to fail at attempting to prevent a murder?"

"You killed her!"

"I did not kill her, you idiot! I didn't kill anyone! I saw the murderer, and if you had brains in your head instead of single-minded dementia, you'd realize that."

"You were seen!"

"Of course I was seen! I was there! I tried to stop it! And I saw the murderer, and if you'd get this blasted blindfold off my face, we could discuss this face to face instead of face to cloth!"

He felt fingers working at the blindfold, and Ryder's angry voice said, "Anna—"

But he was cut short by her infuriated, "Go to hell, Jerry. I mean it. Just go straight to hell."

The blindfold came away, and Chuck blinked in the light.

There was, of course, Anna and Jerry and Joe. And there was Ike, looking plenty steamed. And there was Frank, looking curiously self-satisfied at Chuck's situation. As Chuck had assumed, they were in Ryder and Anna's parlor.

At that moment the door slid open and another conductor, an older man, stepped in. He looked quickly at Ryder, who said evenly, "Jerome Ryder. And you are—?"

"Head conductor Adam Thaler. You got the guy?"

"We know we do, although there are some," and he fired a glance to Anna, "who seem to be under some other impression. Don't worry, though. We've got him under arrest."

"You're some sort of authority?"

"We're with the government."

Thaler shifted uncomfortably. "Do you have any sort of identification?"

"Nothing current," admitted Ryder. "We're with a special division that was created to deal with just such bizarre situations as this. I know I'm asking you to take our word for it—"

"No, no, it's quite all right," said Thaler, putting up his hands. "Better that you handle it than me. The whole thing makes me sick."

"Me, too," said Chuck.

Thaler didn't even look at him, instead turning his gaze away, as if Chuck were something unclean. "Look . . . now that you've got him, I think I better fill you boys in on the whole problem. Before you nailed him, this son of a bitch killed the engineer."

"He did?" said Ryder, appalled. The others looked at Chuck in disgust.

"I did?" Chuck asked. This was just getting better and better.

"Broke his neck."

"So . . . maybe this is a bad question," said Ike slowly, "but who's running the train?"

"It's running itself," said Thaler. "We're just zipping along at 200 miles per hour and no way to slow down. The murderer here rigged the computer so that we can't shut it down."

"Oh that's just great," said Stern

"You got it half-right," said Chuck. He felt almost removed from the discussion. It was so ludicrous it might be happening on another planet. "The murderer rigged it, all right, but he's not here."

"We'll bring him up there and make him fix it," said Ryder firmly.

"Good luck. I know diddly about computers," Chuck told him. Mentally he could have untied the ropes that bound his hands, but he didn't see any point in it. Indeed, the way these guys were looking at him, if he got his hands free, they'd take it as license to shoot him.

Government men? Trained to handle difficult situations? This was just what he needed to make his life miserable.

"You'll know a lot more than diddly, or I swear to God I'll kill you right where you are," said Ike hotly.

"That'll solve a ton, Ike," was Ryder's sour reply. "Conductor, thank you for briefing us. Keep yourself accessible and try to keep the other passengers calm. Let them know that everything is now under control and they are in no danger at all. We'll convince Mr. Simon here that it would be in his best interest to cooperate. He doesn't know how much trouble he's in."

"I'm not the only one," said Chuck sardonically.

The conductor nodded briefly and then left, leaving the

men and woman to look at Chuck with an assortment of expressions ranging from distaste to confusion.

"Now here is what you're going to do," said Ryder, standing over Chuck. He didn't look any too pleased by Chuck's carefully controlled, neutral expression. "You are going to tell us just what you did with the razor weapon that cut poor Rita to pieces. You're going to tell us where you stashed Al's body, because I assume you killed him . . ."

"Jerry," began Anna.

He made a sharp gesture and cut her off. "And then you are going to go up to the front of this train and undo the damage you've done."

"Is that a fact?"

"Yes, Simon, that's a fact."

"Okay," said Chuck. He was amazed at the calm that had settled into his voice. "Now I'll tell you some facts. I did not kill anyone. I did not sabotage this train. What I did do is see the creature that did it, and as long as you've got me tied up like this and spend your time pumping me about things I didn't do, you're giving that monster that much more time to do whatever it wants to whomever it wants."

"You keep talking about a monster, Charlie," Anna said hopefully. She wanted to believe in him. He could tell it. He found it somewhat gratifying. "What kind of monster?"

"Oh, this is bullshit," said Frank Bamberger.

"Its skin was . . . melting in the steam room," said Chuck slowly. "It might not have been a monster, exactly, but some sort of hideous—I don't know—mutation or something."

The men glanced at each other, a brief, disturbed look passing between them. Anna didn't notice it at all.

"He was laughing and snarling," continued Chuck. "He turned the edge of his hand as sharp as a knife. That's how he cut her."

"This is bulllllshit," said Bamberger again in an odd singsong voice.

"Then he changed his appearance. His face—or what passed for a face—transformed into mine. It was probably the most disgusting thing I ever saw. Not quite as disgusting as taking an innocent man and tying him up, but close."

Again the men exchanged looks, and then Ryder's face hardened. "I don't believe it. It's ridiculous."

"Seconded," affirmed Frank.

But Ike was shaking his head. "You know . . . guys . . . it's not impossible. I mean . . ."

"It is impossible," said Bamberger firmly.

"I agree with Ike," said Anna.

Ryder shot her a look. "You don't get a vote."

"I think she's entitled to one," Chuck suggested.

"All right, wise guy," began Ryder

But Anna was speaking fast and furious. "Jerry, you listen to me. I was married to this man. I know what he's capable of and what he isn't. And the cold-blooded murder of a woman he doesn't even know—I refuse to believe it."

"Anna—"

"No! Shut up!" She waved her fists in frustration. "Just shut up! I'm not your little china cup! I know what I'm talking about. You don't know him. I do. And I say that he wouldn't do what you're accusing him of, and if our marriage is going to mean anything at all, then I've got to know that what I say counts for something!"

"It does, Anna, but—"

"No buts. Untie him."

"Anna," said Ryder in frustration.

"I'm untying him," said Stern abruptly. "What she's saying makes sense. There's too much unanswered here."

Ryder paused a moment, and then went to the overhead rack and pulled down a satchel. He reached into it, rummaged around, and removed a handgun that looked like a small truck.

"Jesus," breathed Anna.

He leveled it at Chuck. "All right," he said softly. "Untie him. But if he makes one false move, so help me God, I blow his head off."

"Well that seems eminently fair," said Chuck drily.

Anna went quickly behind him and undid his wrists. He gave her a quick glance as he rubbed them. "Now," said Chuck, "I've told you everything I can."

"Not everything. How did you just happen to show up when this 'monster' was killing Rita?"

My dog told me about it. "You can just chalk that up to luck," said Chuck.

"People make their own luck."

"If that's the case, I wish I'd start making myself some good luck," said Chuck ruefully, "because what I've got so far really stinks. Okay, look, you know about the creature. The skin that melted. The way he changed his appearance. The way he killed your friend—where is she, by the way?"

"Wrapped in plastic and in the cargo section," said Ryder with undisguised distaste. "She'll receive a proper cremation when we reach New York—and so will Al, most likely, when you tell us where you've got him stashed."

"You don't let up, do you?" Chuck observed. He noted with bleak pleasure that even Anna was looking at good old Jerry with undisguised disgust. "Look, Ryder, the sooner we get the obvious out of the way, the better. You're not going to believe anything I say because you're still burned about my past relationship with Anna."

"Wrong." He stabbed a finger at Chuck. "I don't believe anything you say because it all sounds like complete bullshit."

"I left him."

It was Anna who had spoken, and Ryder looked at her in confusion. "What?"

"I left him, okay, Jerry?" said Anna impatiently. "He never did anything to me. I walked out on him because I was a super bitch and wanted to go off on my own. And I was afraid that if I told you what really happened you'd be afraid I'd do the same thing to you."

"Anna, you don't have to stick up for him," said Ryder uncertainly. "Frankly, I don't know what you ever saw in the guy."

"Oh, absolutely," Chuck said readily. "After all, I don't go around waving guns in the face of people who saved my life, or tying them up, or accusing them of murder. I have hardly any redeeming characteristics at all."

"Just shut up, Simon."

"That makes, what, ten times you've said that today?" observed Chuck. He hauled himself up onto the seat next to Anna, flexing his hands to try and restore circulation. "If the words 'shut up' had never been invented, it would cut your conversation time in half."

"Look," Ike Stern said quickly. "Look, Jerry, there's a possibility you're not exploring here."

"He's right," said Arnoff. "That whole thing about someone with flowing skin—"

"Stalker."

It had been Stern who had said it, and the name hung there.

"He's dead," said Ryder firmly.

"What if he's not?"

"I said he's dead."

What if he's not? It was more than just a more forceful question. It was a statement laced with fear. "What if he's on this train? What if he's running around loose?"

"I'll go you one better. What if he's this guy right here,"
said Ryder, pointing his gun at Chuck.

"Jerry, what are you talking about?" said Anna. "Who's
Stalker?"

"If I don't miss my guess," said Chuck slowly, "he's
someone who these guys would rather not see."

"You got that right," said Ike. "He's—"

"Ike," said Ryder threateningly.

Ike Stern fired him a look. "If this guy is Stalker, we're
not telling him anything he doesn't know. If he isn't Stalker,
then he's in this as deep as any of us, and he's entitled to
know what he's up against."

Ryder threw his arms in the air, a clear gesture of being
fed up. It was clear he thought that everyone else had lost
their mind.

Stern turned back to Chuck. "What Jerry was saying
before was true. We do . . . did. . . work for the government. We were an elite strike team. We were sent into all
sorts of dicey situations and pulled off hostage rescues,
terrorist terminations—you name it, we did it. And one of
our people was an operative named Stalker. He had . . .
powers, if you will. Powers that came as a result of a
government experiment. He was incredibly strong. And he
could go practically anywhere. His skin was virtually alive,
so he could alter his appearance by will alone. He developed a talent for mimicking voices as well, so he was
practically indistinguishable from the genuine article. And
about ten years or so ago . . . maybe more, it's hard to
remember . . . we lost him on a mission."

"Lost him?" said Chuck.

"For God's sake, Ike, be honest," said Arnoff. "We lost
him deliberately." He turned to Chuck. "Stalker was
becoming too dangerous. Too unpredictable. The government wanted him gone. We had no choice—we were under

orders. So on one mission, we made sure that Stalker was in the wrong place at the wrong time. He was in a building that blew up—"

"Did you blow it up?" said Chuck.

Pointedly, Arnoff didn't answer. Instead he simply continued, "The last we saw of Stalker was his unmoving body lying in the rubble, and enemy troops closing in on him. Even if he'd been alive, which wasn't remotely likely, then they would have killed him. It couldn't be him now."

"Hell of a coincidence, though, don't you think," said Stern slowly. "This guy, who has no idea of Stalker's existence, gives a fairly accurate description of him."

"Which just helps support that *he's* Stalker," said Ryder.

"Don't be ridiculous," said Anna. "I know Charlie, and this Stalker person doesn't. So there's no way that he could possibly imitate Charlie in such a way that would fool me. It's just not feasible."

"That seems a pretty reasonable assumption to me," said Chuck.

And then Frank spoke in careful, measured tones. "So what you guys are hypothesizing—correct me if I'm wrong here—is that Stalker has returned, obsessed with some sort of need for vengeance. That he's angered that he was left behind and wants to get back at all of us. That he found out about this little gathering, maybe by disguising himself as someone in government and picking up valuable information. And once he did that, he got on board the train for the express purpose of killing everyone in this room."

They shifted uneasily, looking at one another.

"That might pretty much be it," said Ike Stern slowly.

"So what the hell are we going to do about it?" said Arnoff.

"I think," said Chuck slowly, "that I might be able to offer some solution here."

"That being—?" Ryder still looked extremely skeptical and suspicious.

"You'd have to clear it with the conductor, but I might have a way of tracking down Stalker—presuming that he's disguised himself as someone else."

"What would you do?"

"I've got a dog," said Chuck. "He's currently in the baggage compartment. I think he could detect Stalker."

"Now how in hell do you know that?" Ryder wasn't making this remotely easy.

Chuck saw nothing but trouble in trying to explain that Rommel had psychic abilities. Because, naturally, he'd have to explain about his own as well, and that was definitely not going to go over well with this group. "Because he has an incredibly keen sense of smell," he said. "And once we put him on the track, he'll be able to lead us right to Stalker. He's not going to be fooled by physical appearance, because the scent isn't going to change."

"I hate to say it, but it sounds really reasonable," said Arnoff. Stern was nodding as well.

"I still don't trust him," said Ryder.

"You don't have to trust him implicitly, Jerry," said Frank. "After all, it's not like you're marrying him. Your fiancée already did that." That comment won him a nasty look from Ryder, although to Chuck's surprise, Anna chuckled softly.

"Ike," said Ryder after a moment, "go clear it with the conductor."

"You mean the one we just told that we had the killer all squared away," said Stern. "Oh, he's just going to love that."

"You're the smooth talker, Ike. You'll make him understand, and he'll even thank you for it."

"Thanks," said Stern sourly, and walked out of the parlor.

"While he's doing that," said Chuck after a moment, "would you mind terribly if I returned to my parlor to tell the young lady I was with just what's going on? I mean, I sort of vanished into thin air. It's not especially polite, and considering that she's probably heard by now that people are getting killed on this train, she might think that I was one of the victims."

"You mean, just like Anna, she knows you're so wonderful that you couldn't possibly be the killer?" asked Ryder.

Chuck smiled ingratiatingly. "That's right."

"All right," said Ryder evenly. "But I'm going to come with you. Keep an eye on you."

"What should *we* do?" asked Arnoff.

"Take a walk through the train," Ryder told them. "Just a routine patrol. Make sure that nothing whacked is going on. And maybe, God help us, you'll find Al's body."

They nodded and stood. Anna and Chuck went out into the hallway, and Ryder was about to follow when Frank Bamberger said, "Hey, Jerry . . . how do we know that one of us isn't Stalker?"

His face set, Ryder said, "Because I got this gut feeling that there's still something hinky about this Simon guy. I know he's staging this whole cooperation thing, but it's too pat. Y'know? Something about him is setting off the old internal warning system. Either he's the murderer, or if it is Stalker responsible, then this guy is Stalker, or at least knows more than he's telling. I'd be willing to stake my life on it."

"That, Jerry," said Frank, "may be exactly what you're doing."

8

CHUCK AND ANNA walked slowly down the corridor, with Jerome Ryder following several steps behind. He now had the gun tucked away in his jacket, but you would have had to be a blind man not to see the bulge in the line. Its presence was not lost on the terrified passengers who peered out from their parlors as the cautious trio walked past them. Chuck couldn't help but notice that he left a string of muttered "That's the bastard. That's the guy who did it" in his wake. All things considered, he realized, it might not have been a bad idea that they were keeping an eye on him. He could probably use the protection from the mob mentality surrounding him.

In a low voice he said to Anna, "Pardon my asking but . . . just what do you see in this guy, anyway?"

A small smile crept across her face. "Guess it's kind of hard to see it, huh?"

"I've love to get a close look, but his gun's in the way."

"He's strong," she said after a moment. "He's very assertive. Very knowledgeable. Knows very much what he

wants and how he's going to go about it. Very protective
and considerate of me."

"When he's not telling you to shut up."

"Oh, you're as bad as he is, you know that?" she said.
"He's a good man. He really is. He's told me some of the
things he was involved with when he and the other people
you saw were part of a government strike team. He's led a
life, Charlie, that you can't even begin to imagine."

"My imagination can run pretty wild sometimes," said
Chuck.

"I feel . . . safe when I'm with him. Safe and secure
that he'll protect me and support me in whatever it is I want
to do."

"And I wasn't able to offer you that?" asked Chuck in
surprise.

"Not the same way. We were both too young, Charlie,
you and I. He's an older man . . ."

"I noticed."

"And I find that very comforting in a way. I draw
strength from that, and he draws strength from my youth."

"Well how symbiotic can you get?"

Her eyes flushed. "You sound jealous."

"Jealous? Me? Nah. My wife is going to be marrying a
man who has a gun trained on me because he thinks I'm a
rampaging, murdering monster. How could I help but love
a guy like that?"

"You're not seeing him at his best."

"I'm sorry. Next time I'll be sure to bring a flag so he can
salute it."

They lapsed into silence until they were in front of
Chuck's parlor. He knocked and, upon hearing the worried
voice of Sandy Sendak saying, "Yes," slid open the door.

Sandy saw him and shrieked.

Chuck slid the door closed and turned back to Anna. "I

don't usually have this effect on women. You're not seeing me at my best. Usually they try and rip my clothes off instead of shaking hands."

"Oh, I know. I know."

He opened the door and forced a smile. "Hi. I thought you might—"

Then he ducked back as an ashtray sailed across the room and narrowly avoided clunking him in the head. A cautionary TK push away made sure that the ashtray missed him, but it was the thought that counted.

He glanced at Anna and said evenly, "This could take a few minutes."

"Fine. I have all the time in the world."

"Don't we all."

Frank Bamberger stuck his head into the room labeled GYMNASIUM and uttered a curt laugh. "Check this out, Arn," he called. "I swear, this place has everything."

Joe Arnoff came in behind him, looking faintly annoyed. "Frank, this isn't really the time. We're supposed to be looking over the train—"

Frank was walking through the small but efficient gym. There was a handful of electronic weight machines and, just for the sake of nostalgia, an old-style bench-press universal gym.

"You want my opinion, Arn? I don't think we have to look any farther. I think we already nailed the son of a bitch."

"You mean that Simon guy? But—"

"Doesn't that make a lot more sense than that Stalker suddenly showed up out of nowhere? I mean, let's get real with each other, Arn. The guy's dead. He's wormfood. I don't know, maybe Simon is demented enough to believe what he's saying and he's just seen too many late night movies." He patted the bench press. "You used to be the group strong man, Arn, in addition to being the resident, tight-ass. Still think you've got what it takes."

"Frank, this is really ridiculous—"

Bamberger pointed a teasing finger at him. "Dinner on me says you can't bench your own weight."

Arnoff allowed a flicker of annoyance to cross his normally stoic face. "You're really asking for it, you know that?"

Frank held his hands out to his side in an inviting pose. "Then give it to me, sport."

Looking around as if he were concerned that someone was watching them—not especially likely, since virtually all of the passengers were cowering in their parlors—Arnoff removed his jacket and lay down on the red leather bench. He slid up, positioning himself under the grips. "So you really think that this Simon guy did it? But then how did he do it? Where's the razor that he used to cut Rita up? Hell, her right arm was severed—he practically would have had to use a chain saw or something."

"I've got an even better one for you," said Bamberger. He leaned against the universal gym and studied his fingernails in a faintly distracted manner. "What if Simon is more than he seems?"

"Meaning?" Joe half-turned on his back to study the weights that were stacked behind him. He reached over and pulled out the latch peg, a small metal piece that was inserted into holes within the weights so that weight lifter could determine how much he was going to attempt to press. He moved it farther down on the weight stacks so that he would be pressing 150 to start out. He didn't want to admit how long it had been since he had done any serious working out, but at the same time he didn't want to rupture his spine because of some misplaced sense of machismo.

"You know how Jerry says the government's interested in the return of SPEAR in order to deal with runaway psionics and the like?"

"Yeah." Arnoff reached up and grasped the grips firmly. He inhaled and exhaled rapidly four times and then, holding his breath, pushed upward. The stack of weights directly behind his head lifted up, clearing a space easily. He held it there, satisfied that it wasn't much of a problem, and then lowered it. Turning over to increase the weight up to 180, he said, "What's your point? You're thinking that this Chuck Simon guy could be one of the psionics we're on the lookout for?"

"Possible," said Bamberger. "Remember the name of the psionic that Jerry said we're supposed to be going after?"

"I think he called him . . . what . . . Psi-Man?"

"That's right." He paused. "Pretty close similarity in names, wouldn't you say?"

Arnoff frowned. "That's a real stretch, Frank. I mean it, that really is." He huffed and puffed a few more quick times and then raised up the weights once more. He was now pressing 180. His arms were trembling as he held it, but he did, his mouth set and determined. Then he lowered them, and they fell with a resounding clang.

"Not bad," said Bamberger, impressed.

Arnoff grinned. "You owe me dinner, hotshot. I'd like to see you do better than that."

"Oh yeah? Just stay where you are." Frank reached over, removed the latch peg, and inserted in into the weight slot that read 260 pounds.

"You're nuts," said Arnoff with one of his rare grins. "You'll never lift that." He started to get up from the bench, and suddenly Bamberger had planted his foot squarely on Arnoff's chest. Arnoff angrily tried to sit up, but Bamberger kept him squarely pinned to the bench. "What're you, fuckin' crazy!" bellowed Arnoff. "Let me up, Frank! I mean it!"

"Here's the bit, Arn, old buddy, old pal," Frank told him, his voice not evincing any sign of strain as he kept Arnoff firmly in place. "I happen to know for a fact that Simon is Psi-Man. I just wanted to share that with you."

"Okay, fine, now let me the hell up, you jerk!"

"Poor, poor Arn," said Bamberger sadly. "You were always the one who was so serious. The tight-ass, just like we always kidded you. Always had the weight of the world on your shoulders."

"Goddammit, Frank—"

"Not Frank." He reached out and, with one hand, lifted up the 260 pounds of weight. Arnoff gasped as he saw it, and then Frank shoved him forward. Arnoff's head went directly into the gap created by the lifted weights, and he looked straight up at the gleaming metal of the bottom weight. A face filled with terror was reflected in it. Pointed directly toward his head also was the weight bar, a downward-projecting shaft of metal which had lifted completely out of the receptacles.

"No, not Frank," continued the man who effortlessly held up the weight. "Stalker." He released the weights.

Arnoff's scream was truncated by the weights as they dropped obediently back into place. The weight bar struck him first, drilling straight through his head, and it was followed a split instant later by the actual weights that clanged down, crushing his entire skull. Fluids oozed from between the weights and dripped to the floor.

Stalker took a step back and smiled his death's head grin. And then he suddenly frowned. He sensed something, something animallike. Something aware of him, brushing across his mind, howling fury and a challenge.

He had been vaguely aware of it before, but now it was

even more clear. The humans were all meat, but this other thing . . . this other thing presented a danger. Stalker growled low in his throat and went in search of the danger, to eliminate it once and for all.

"Sandy, it wasn't me," said Chuck, trying to sound as patient as he could.

She wasn't buying any of it. "I saw you!" she said from the far end of the parlor. "I saw them dragging you past! People said you were some sort of murderer! You'd killed a woman, maybe other people! They said—"

"Sandy, listen to me," he said. It would almost have been funny if it weren't so damned frustrating. "If I were really some crazed murderer—why are you still alive?"

"What do you mean?"

"I mean we spent time alone together, right here, in this parlor," he said reasonably. "Did I make any threatening move toward you?"

"Well . . . no," she admitted.

"Any gesture? Make you feel in any way as if you were in danger?"

Again, "Well . . . no."

"Did I sound at all murderous?"

"Actually, you sounded kind of pathetic."

"Oh," he said. "Well—"

"In fact, you even got a little whiny—"

"A simple 'no' would have sufficed," he said impatiently.

"But then, why did—?"

"Because the murderer bears a passing resemblance to me, that's all," Chuck said. "It was a case of—"

Suddenly Chuck's entire body went tense. He got a faraway look in his eyes, and Sandy took an apprehensive step back. She had just been starting to believe him, but

now it suddenly looked as if he were going to throw some
sort of psychotic fit. "Sy—?" she said, still under the
impression his name was Simon Charles.

"Oh my God," he whispered. And, Sandy Sendak
completely forgotten, he turned and grabbed for the door.

Just outside the door, Ryder was standing impatiently
next to Anna, and he muttered in a low voice, "You know,
frankly, I don't know what you ever saw in the guy."

"Funny," she said in faintly amused tone. "He said more
or less the same thing about you. I bet if you gave each
other a chance you'd get along great."

"Never happen."

And suddenly the door was hurled aside. Ryder immediately brought his gun up, more out of reflex than anything
else, but the speed of the gesture startled Anna, and she let
out a small shriek.

Chuck was standing in the doorway, his eyes wild, and he
shouted, *"He's after Rommel! He's after Rommel!"*

"Who is?" demanded Ryder. "Who's Rommel? Who's
after him?"

"My dog! Stalker's after my dog!"

"How do you—"

His question went unanswered, because Chuck charged
directly toward him. Actually, he was trying to get past
him, but Ryder was stubbornly blocking the way. "Hold it,
Simon! You're not going anywhere before I—"

Burning with cold fury that the single-minded Ryder was
getting in his way, Chuck simply hurled him aside with a
mild swipe of his TK. Ryder stumbled back and hit the
ground, gasping in shock and surprise. Chuck vaulted over
him and charged down the corridor, Anna and Sandy
shouting after him.

Ryder brought his gun up, ready to fire, but he saw the
way Anna was looking at him and suddenly realized just

how much he wanted to shoot Simon, and just how much Anna would hate him for it if he did in any situation other than self-defense. Shooting the fleeing Simon in the leg was perfectly acceptable to Ryder, but he had the distinct feeling that he might very well lose Anna over it. Women just didn't understand about these kinds of things.

He clambered to his feet, shouted Chuck's name, and started off after him.

Rommel was shouting an alarm in Chuck's mind. *He just killed again. I can sense it. And now he's coming after me.*

"I'm coming!" Chuck shouted. "Don't worry!"

I'm not worried. I can handle him.

"From inside a cage?! He could stand ten feet away and shoot you!"

There was a momentary pause, and then Rommel said, *Maybe you'd better come, just the same.*

Word having spread around that the killer had been captured, passengers had started finding the nerve to venture out of their cabins despite advice to the contrary. Now, though, seeing Chuck charging their way, they started shouting and screaming and trying to get out of his path. The only result was a chaotic crowd in front of him, and Chuck hurled himself into it with abandon and barely controlled fury. It was like swimming through quicksand as he shoved with his arms and his TK, scooping people out of the way and hurling them aside. He went through them like a one-man flying wedge, shoving and pushing, trying to get back to the baggage car where Rommel was. And right behind him, catching up, was Ryder, followed by Anna. Sandy had wisely decided to stay back in her cabin.

Trainee conductor Richard Goldstein saw Chuck coming, saw the confusion and panic that was ensuing. He knew that he should be doing something to stop it, but his mind locked. This was supposed to be a nice, simple job. Take tickets, tell the passengers endlessly how long it would be until they arrived at the destination, and occasionally direct the maintenance crew in cleaning up if somebody got sick. That was it. This, with murderers and bodies and hysteria, it was all too much.

He decide to withdraw, and stepped into the first place that seemed to get him out of the way of the brouhaha. He yanked open the door of the gym and started to step inside.

That was when he spotted the maimed body, with the head crushed beneath the weights. It was entirely too much for him, but Richard Goldstein managed to stammer out, "I resign," before collapsing in a dead faint.

9

STALKER, STILL WEARING the image of Frank Bamberger, slid open the door that was marked BAGGAGE CAR, and bore the warning beneath that of AUTHORIZED PERSONNEL ONLY. He smiled inwardly. Only authorized personnel. My, my. He might get himself into trouble someday if he continued to flagrantly violate such important rules as that.

He stepped into the dimness of the freight car and slid the door shut behind him, waiting for his eyes to adjust. The car was the only one in the train that was windowless, although he could make out that there was a door at the far end. It had a blacked-over window set into the upper half.

And then, from there in the darkness, he heard a growling.

"You're the one, aren't you?" said Stalker. "You're the one I've felt tickling against the back of my head."

Rommel barked and snapped fiercely. Stalker stood his ground, now able to make out the large cage that contained the infuriated animal. He let out a low whistle. "You're a big son of a bitch—no offense intended. But then, that wouldn't exactly be offensive to you, now, would it."

The German shepherd charged forward, slamming against the door. It creaked dangerously, the hinges trying their best to hang on. The animal hurled its full weight against it a second, third, and fourth time, and Stalker stood there, grinning, shaking his head. "You're really going crazy in there, aren't you. You know something? You're the only one with brains on this whole damned train. Kind of a pity you couldn't be my dog. We'd make one hell of a team."

Stalker flattened his hands and the edges acquired razor hardness. They were the same texture and deadliness that they had been when he had carved pretty Rita, Meter Maid, to bits. He hoped that she and good old Al were happy together, burning in hell.

He moved around the cage to try and get in a good shot at the dog. The animal turned around, but its movement was hampered by the relative smallness of the cage. It was growling and barking furiously, trying to keep its dangerous jaws facing Stalker while snapping at him.

Stalker grinned. The animal might as well do his work for him. "Come on, doggie," he said, taking a step back, drawing his hand over his head. "Come and get me."

The dog shoved his face through the bars, his huge maw snapping and snarling at Stalker. His entire muzzle was extended through the bars, although he was unable to fit any more of his head through. That was going to be more than enough for Stalker, who prepared to bring his hand whistling down and slice the dog's muzzle off. He couldn't wait for the creature's reaction when it realized that the front half of its head was lying on the floor, an impotent piece of bone and teeth. The dog would try to bark, or course, or yelp, or do something, but none of that would be possible since its mouth would be gone. Then he'd watch it bleed to death, or maybe he would help it along. Put doggie to sleep permanently.

His hand started to move, and then the door to the luggage compartment clanged open once more. Stalker looked up in annoyance, and then annoyance switched to faint alarm, because Psi-Man was standing there, his hands balled into fists, his face twisted in fury.

Stalker moved around the cage quickly to the far end of the car, his immediate instinct to put as much distance between himself and Chuck Simon as he could. He then realized, as he stood with his back to the door at the far end, that this was a mistake. Distance favored Simon. But Stalker wasn't without his own resources, and even as Chuck Simon paused a moment to try and get a sense of the room, Stalker had reached into his sleeve and pulled out a throwing knife. With one smooth motion he hurled it directly at Simon.

Chuck sensed it at the last second and half-twisted to get out of its way. If he hadn't then, it would have thudded squarely into his chest, stabbing him in the heart. As it was, it struck him instead in the upper arm—relatively harmless in comparison to the damage it could have done, but it still hurt like hell. Chuck let out a yell and staggered back, and Stalker started toward him.

Simon hurled his right hand forward as if delivering a fastball, and it was pure instinct that prompted Stalker to suddenly hit the ground. It saved his life, for a TK bolt passed invisibly over his head and blew apart the blacked-over window of the opposite door with such force and power that Stalker suddenly realized that the Psi-Man wasn't just fucking around anymore.

At that moment, with a final howl of pure fury, the berserk German shepherd hurled its massive body against the door of its prison. The hinges gave way with a protesting screech of metal, and the door crashed to the ground as Rommel exploded into the confines of the luggage car. The first thing the dog encountered was a large hanging bag, which he clamped in his jaws and ripped to shreds in his frenzy, as if warming up for getting to Stalker.

It was at that point that Stalker became aware that hanging around might not be such a hot idea.

Thought became action, and in a flash Stalker had climbed through the busted glass of the door and was outside the train, standing on a small platform, not more than three feet wide.

The wind and speed of the train roared around him as he dropped to the floor of the platform. The dropping motion had been a second's work, a well-spent second, as it turned out, when the air crackled over his head, and he realized that another TK blast had just leaped over his head. He didn't want to know what would happen if one of those things struck him, but he had the feeling that he would be able to turn around and watch his internal organs decorate the landscape of Kansas or Missouri—wherever the hell it was that they were now.

His skin was already freeforming around him, and he willed it to additional oozing cohesion as he yanked off his socks and shoes. Even as, for psychological advantage, he transformed his face into Simon's image again, he reached out to the side of the train. His fingers adhered, and a second later, he brought his feet up as well, clambering upward like a fly or a spider, with a series of rapid-fire *spluch* sounds. The wind blew past him, and he had to be careful not to make a misstep, because otherwise he would be tossed right off the train by the blasting wind.

Inside the car, Chuck grabbed Rommel by the muzzle. "Did he hurt you! Are you okay?!"

I'm fine! He's getting away!

"I'm after him!" He started for the door.

Get him, Chuck.

Chuck tossed a surprise glance at the dog. Rommel rarely, if ever, called him by name. The great canine had made abundantly clear the total disdain he held for such human affectations. "I'll get him," Chuck affirmed.

Once again the door slid open, and then Ryder was there, his gun out, and he was shouting, "Hold it, Simon! Don't move a muscle!"

Rommel, partially obscured by a trunk, glanced at Chuck. *Who is this idiot? Should I just kill him?*

For the most fleeting of moments, Chuck entertained the notion, but then dismissed it. "He's no threat, Rommel. Just entertain him. Ryder! He went out this way, and I'm going after him!" He gritted his teeth and yanked the bloody knife from his arm, dropping the weapon to the floor.

"You're going nowhere." And Ryder drew the hammer of his gun back.

Chuck froze the hammer with his mind as Rommel charged forward, barking furiously. Ryder's eyes went wide with terror as he brought his gun around and aimed it at the infuriated dog, but he couldn't make it fire.

"That's Rommel! Don't aim guns at him, and he'll be nice to you! He's the only sure way we have of tracking the killer, and if I don't nail him now, we won't have a prayer of getting him later."

Then, for good measure, Chuck gave a TK push that sent Ryder sprawling and, while doing so, nudged the gun from his grasp. It slid across the floor safely into a corner out of Ryder's reach. Rommel stood in between the man and his gun, snarling.

"Be nice and he won't rip your arm off," Chuck said as his parting shot, and then stepped out onto the platform.

He stood there for a moment, looking around, and then some instinct warned him at the last second and he ducked. There was a swift motion just over his head, and he glanced up in time to see his own face staring down at him—and a razor-sharp hand sweeping past in a barely missed chop.

Chuck fired back with a TK burst, and Stalker ducked away, heading back along the roof of the train.

Chuck had never gotten the hang of levitating himself and approximating flying, but he had acquired a knack for using his TK ability to push off from a surface and give himself an extra jump. That was what he endeavored to do now. Crouching, he sprung upward, using his TK power to give an additional push against the platform so that he could land squarely on the roof of the train.

For one second he was suspended in the air, in contact with neither the roof nor the platform, and he reached out to snag the roof.

In performing the maneuver, Chuck Simon had forgotten one thing.

Both he and the train were moving at 200 miles per hour, but the moment he broke contact with the train, he began to slow down while the Bullet Train maintained its breakneck pace. As a result, when he tried to land on the top of the train, it wasn't there anymore. The train was hurtling away, and Chuck was staring straight down at the blur of track beneath him.

Realizing his mistake didn't do him a damn bit of good as Chuck started to fall, moving at a significantly fast enough speed that they would be able to scrape him up with a spatula for weeks to come once he hit the ground.

Stalker, perched on the roof half a car length away, adhering with the uncanny suction of his hands and feet, laughed hysterically at the incredibly stupid move of the Psi-Man. Here he had been concerned about the guy posing some sort of threat, and instead he'd gone and graciously eliminated himself.

Chuck did the only thing he could. In desperation, he

reached out with his mind and gripped the end of the last train car. There was no way in hell, of course, that Chuck had the power to force the train itself to come to a halt. So instead the train continued at 200 miles per hour and dragged the desperate Psi-Man behind it. He held on, his only support an invisible line of psionic force stretching from deep within the frantic reaches of his own mind.

He held on, straining, his mind feeling like it was going to split. The ground was an indistinguishable blur beneath him, the wind roaring in his ears. The train itself was eerily silent, giving the whole situation a dreamlike quality.

Chuck sailed along behind the train, his arms outstretched, looking like a human airplane. He was suspended barely four feet from the ground.

It felt as if it was everything he could do simply to avoid letting go, but he had to do more than that if he was going to extricate himself from the situation. Gritting his teeth, he told his mind to start pulling the train toward himself. He couldn't do it, of course, but it was a way of tricking his own mind into doing what he wanted. The train started to inch closer toward him, but, in fact, he was pulling himself closer to the train, as if dragging himself hand over hand along a trailing rope. Except this trailing rope was created by the pure force and determination of his own mind.

He dragged himself closer and closer, and he saw, up on the roof, a creature with his own face, dark and distorted, laughing at him. If it was meant to distract him, to rattle him so that he would lose his grip and fall off the train, go tumbling end over end and smear across the track—all it actually did was strengthen his resolve. He approached the train with unflagging determination, his jaw set, his mind bubbling with rage and fury.

The Chaos Kid, the poor, confused lad that he had faced in San Francisco, had been a sick and troubled young man.

But Stalker—he was a vindictive psychopath. Chuck took all of the anger that boiled within himself and channeled it into greater strength of mind than ever before.

Stalker stepped back in surprise as Simon was now only a few feet away from the edge of the roof. He considered getting close to the edge and trying to swipe at the Psi-Man as soon as he got within range. But something in the expression on Simon's face warned Stalker that this not only had the makings of a bad idea, it was potentially a fatal idea.

So instead he turned and ran. Actually, he didn't run so much as move crablike down the length of the train, his hands and feet making suction cuplike noises.

Right after him came the Psi-Man, who followed him on the roof, arms at either side, balancing like a tightrope walker. Chuck had picked up a few tips in that noble profession from a woman named Dakota when he'd spent time in the circus. Of course, it also helped that he was using his TK power to anchor himself to the roof of the car, gripping it with the full strength of his mind.

Unfortunately, doing that made it impossible for Chuck to take any sort of offensive action against Stalker. It was all he could do to keep an eye on him and keep him on the defensive.

Stalker proceeded cautiously, not wanting to move too quickly for fear of being tossed right off the train. That he would be killed seemed a secondary concern to the notion that the remaining members of SPEAR would get away. Not that there were many remaining. Only Ike Stern and Jerome Ryder were left. And maybe he'd dispose of Ryder's bitch as well.

And then he heard the pounding of feet behind him and risked a look around. To his shock, Simon was now directly behind him. He was moving with daredevil abandon, and he

leaped the gap from the rear car to the next car on which
Stalker was perched, snaring it with his psi power and
landing cleanly. Now he was standing, crouched, a mere
few feet away.

For a moment Stalker wondered why Simon didn't
simply push him off the train with the power of his mind. It
never occurred to Stalker that it might be because Chuck
had no desire to kill him since killing was anathema to
Psi-Man.

The only thing that Stalker could come up with—and it
seemed quite reasonable, really—was that Chuck needed to
show up with Stalker in hand to prove his own innocence.
There was, indeed, some validity to this view, and it gave
Stalker a measure of hope. Even a sort of swaggering
confidence.

He didn't realize that Chuck was using everything he had,
in terms of his TK power, to keep his place on the speeding
train. That Chuck couldn't lash out with a psi bolt, as much
as he wanted to, or even spare a portion of his power to
hammerlock the assassin.

Chuck squinted, the wind fierce in his face, and then
Stalker charged at him. He came toward him spiderlike, a
rapid succession of suction cup sounds, and then risked
letting go with both hands, focusing all of his sticking
ability on his feet. He thrust forward a hand fashioned into
spear sharpness.

Chuck stepped back with one foot, allowing Stalker to
deplete the thrust of his forward motion, treating Stalker's
thrust as if he had a knife in his hand. He tried to ignore the
numb feeling he was getting in his left arm, thanks to the
blood that was flowing from the wound there. Then he
grabbed Stalker's forearm, trying to twist it around so that
he could immobilize it. Send Stalker to his knees, maybe
even knock him unconscious.

The forearm rippled beneath his grasp, and Chuck held on with dogged determination, trying to grasp the bone so that no matter how much the skin undulated, he wouldn't lose his grip.

And then the skin of the forearm re-formed razor sharp across Chuck's palm, slicing his hand. With a yell of surprise and pain, Chuck yanked backward—and lost his psionic grip on the train.

He tumbled down the length of the car, and rolled over the gap between the car they'd been on and the last car of the train. His fingers snagged the edge of the last car, and he gripped it desperately, regaining his equilibrium. He lay flat on the last car, reaching out with the power of his mind and stabilizing himself, and then he looked ahead of him to the car he'd just been on.

Stalker was now two cars ahead and moving fast, scrambling like a train-hopping crab.

With a howl of frustration, Chuck slammed a fist down and scrambled to his feet. He steadied himself with his TK and then took off after Stalker once more.

Stalker glanced over his shoulder, saw Chuck coming toward him, incredibly fast. Two cars away. Stalker made it another few feet and then Simon was right behind him, with fury in his eyes and murder in his heart.

Stalker glanced to his right and saw the metal rods that ran along the edge of the train—the ones designed primarily as decorative hand grips for maintenance men. Anchoring himself firmly, and with Simon closing in on him, he reached out with one hand and grabbed the rod firmly. He yanked hard, and a length of rod about five feet snapped free. He stood quickly, the wind screaming and threatening to hurl him off, and swung the rod around at Simon.

Simon dropped flat to the roof of the car, clutching on with all his strength, and turned his TK on Stalker, trying to knock the rod from his hands. But Stalker's grip was superhuman, and Chuck couldn't knock the bar free.

Then Stalker came at him, reversing his grip and smashing the bar down. Chuck rolled to one side, skidded across the polished metal, and slid off the train.

His fingers lashed out, and he grabbed a fragment of the iron bar that remained attacked to the train. He clung to the side of the Bullet Train, legs pumping, trying to clamber to the top once more.

With a heart-stopping creak of metal, the iron bar bent in its bracing. Chuck swung outward at a 90-degree angle to the train, clutching on desperately, his arms straining. He tried to ignore the numbness in his arm that was making it practically impossible to hang on, because the alternative to hanging on was falling off.

Sandy Sendak heard some sort of commotion overhead. She glanced out the window of the parlor and saw the man she knew as Simon Charles dangling nearby, holding onto a piece of iron bar, his left arm covered with blood.

Naturally she screamed.

Hand over hand, Chuck started making his way back toward the train car. The bar creaked dangerously, threatening to snap off, and then he saw Stalker crouched atop the car, laughing and pointing. Against his better judgment, Chuck glanced where Stalker was indicating.

Far ahead, but coming up fast, was a tunnel dug through the side of a small mountain. It would be there in less than an eyeblink.

Stalker hurled himself flat, keeping the bar out in front of him and he tossed off a farewell wave to Chuck, who, in no time at all, was going to be smeared outside the entrance of the tunnel.

Frantically, Chuck hurled his bodyweight forward and
mentally yanked himself toward the train. The bar creaked
one final time and, just as they reached the tunnel, snapped.
Chuck slammed against the side of the train, and his right
hand snared out and snagged one of the bar braces.

Darkness enveloped him, whizzing past in a blur of
blackness, and he felt as if he were on a one-way ticket ride
to hell. In the blackness of the tunnel, though, Stalker
couldn't do anything. He was hugging the top of the train,
afraid to rise for fear of being killed. The wall of the tunnel
was bare inches away from him as, with an additional push
via his TK, Chuck propelled himself up to the top of the
train. He lay there, panting a moment, and then his respite
was over as the train broke out into daylight. It was then that
Chuck discovered, somewhat to his surprise, that he was
still clutching the section of iron bar that had snapped off.
It was slightly shorter than what Stalker was holding, but
serviceable.

He looked up and saw Stalker just a few feet away,
regarding him with something akin to amazement. Then
Stalker crept forward, his feet suction-cupping behind him,
raising up the bar over his head.

Chuck mentally anchored himself to the train once more,
his back to the howling wind, and held the rod crosswise.
Stalker's bar crashed down with a clang, but Chuck blocked
it with his own.

They locked against each other, trying to muscle each
other off with sheer weight and determination. Then Stalker
stepped back, *spluch*, *spluch*, holding the bar evenly with
both hands and then he swung it like a quarterstaff.

Chuck had had some experience with staff techniques,
but not a lot. Stalker looked far more proficient, but every
move was laced with caution and fighting against the wind
and speed of the train.

Stalker swung low, a shot designed to smash across Chuck's leg, maybe even break his knee. Chuck caught it, shoved Stalker's iron staff upward and swung the bottom of his own around. He caught Stalker squarely in the pit of his stomach, the jagged edge of the staff cutting across Stalker's belly. Stalker roared in fury and brought his staff around from the right. Chuck partially blocked it, but the staff skidded down the length of his own and mashed the fingers of his right hand.

Then the staves moved quickly, Stalker mostly on the offensive, trying to drive in hard and strike Chuck down. But to the fury of the assassin, Simon blocked his every thrust, parried his every attempted strike. Always at the last second, and always by the slimmest of margins. The clanging of the makeshift weapons and the grunts of the combatants—combatants who looked remarkably like each other—dueling with staves atop the speeding Bullet Train was an amazing spectacle to which there were no witnesses.

Stalker swung his staff crosswise, hoping to catch Chuck off guard. Chuck abruptly thrust his entire body out of the way and slammed a fist into Stalker's face. It left a massive indentation in the pliable skin, and Stalker's face began to coalesce and re-form into a visage with no discernible features, but utterly grotesque nonetheless in his inhumanity. For just a moment, the ungodly transformation did what Stalker's maneuvering had been unable to do—it caught Chuck flatfooted.

Stalker changed his angle and footing and thrust down hard, shoving the point of Chuck's staff downward. He head-butted Chuck, and that alone was almost enough to break Chuck's concentration and send him tumbling from the train.

Chuck went to one knee, gripping his staff, and Stalker took a step toward him, momentarily straddling Chuck's staff. Gripping the staff as hard as he could, Chuck shoved upward and sent the end slamming up between Stalker's legs.

Stalker screamed, pain exploding behind his eyes, and he staggered back, losing his grip on the rod and, not only that, his suction-hold on the train. He tumbled back and off to the side, opposite where Chuck had fallen mere moments before, and now it was Stalker who clutched on desperately to one of the rods that remained attached to the train.

Unlike the Psi-Man, however, Stalker had had quite enough. Dangling in front of a window, he kicked out with his foot and smashed it in. From inside he heard the angry shout of a man and the startled scream of a woman, and then he swung his body in and landed with a faint, disgusting *squish* sound.

Amusement flashed through his mind, because he'd dropped in rather unexpectedly on a man and woman who had been about to embark on a roll in the hay. The shrieking woman was wrapped up in a sheet, lying on a parlor couch that had been opened up into a bed—a narrow fit but not an impossible one. The bed was now covered with glass from Stalker's rather abrupt entrance.

Standing nearby, wearing jockey shorts with a noticeable bulge, was a man with a long face and a short temper. "Who the *hell* are *you*!?" he shouted, starting toward Stalker.

Stalker came up from his crouch, his face a shifting mass of revulsion, his fingers already forming into talons. The man stopped in his tracks halfway across the bed, and the woman, peering out from under the sheets, screamed the man's name. Stalker, infuriated over how badly things were going, had no patience at all. He swung his hand forward, opening the man up from crotch to sternum, and took some measure of solace in the man's expression, as the unfortunate victim promptly showed what he was made of by having it all spill out on the floor in front of them.

He spun, facing the woman, whose face had gone deathly white and who looked ready to vomit. As the man fell silently to the floor, accompanied by a fairly loud *squish*, Stalker took a step toward the woman, his hand drawn back.

"You think *you're* having a bad day?" he demanded. "Look at it from my point of view."

And at that moment Chuck Simon, with timing bordering on the supernatural, swung in through the smashed window.

His foot hit he-didn't-know-what on the floor (and was probably the better for not knowing), and he skidded slightly before catching himself. Then he realized what he was standing on, and Stalker seized the momentary distraction to leap straight at Chuck. The quarters were too confined for Chuck to make good use of his aikido, and his mind was too numbed by the horrors he was witnessing to reach out with his TK powers.

He was no virgin to horror. In his time on the run, he had seen violence and brutality that sickened the heart and blackened the soul. But he had never seen anyone—not even the assassin known as Beutel—who was as relentlessly, cavalierly, bloodthirsty as this creature called Stalker.

Stalker slammed into Chuck, Chuck barely managing to react in time to snag his wrists and spread them wide. They tumbled backward onto the bed, a problem made even greater by the fact that the woman was still in it. She screeched directly into Chuck's ear, which helped even less.

They struggled in the bed, and there was no art or skill to what Chuck was doing now. Plain and simple, he was pounding on Stalker's face, smashing the already-unrecognizable mass into an even greater pile of sludge. The woman, still shrieking, was trying to get out of the bed, but she became tangled up in the sheets and was yanked into the middle of the brawl.

The edges of Stalker's hands were once again honed, and he tried to bring them across Chuck's neck. But Chuck moved too quickly, yanking his head out of the way, and Stalker's hand sliced across the cushion.

With a roar, Chuck lashed out with his TK once more, concentrating it on Stalker, and he shoved him away so hard that Stalker hurled back out the window of the car.

"*Aw no!*" shouted Chuck, who was not remotely looking forward to crawling around outside the train again. He ran to the window, stuck his head out, and suddenly yanked it back as fast as he could when he realized just what a target he was presenting.

It was fortunate that he did, because Stalker's taloned hand sliced down from just overhead, whisking barely an inch away from Chuck's neck. Chuck dropped to the floor and angled his head so he could see out the window without exposing himself to attack. What he saw was Stalker clambering away up the side of the train and then out of his sight line.

"No No *No!*" Chuck roared, unable to believe this was happening. He ran out the parlor, ignoring the screams of the girl.

Across the way, Sandy was standing in the doorway shouting, "Sy, what's happening?!" And to Chuck's right, he heard more screaming and chaos heading his way up the aisle. People were falling over each other to get out of the way as Rommel pounded up the aisle toward him, with good old Jerry Ryder shoving his way through from behind.

"Simon!" bellowed Ryder. "We're gonna talk, you and I!"

"You talk! I'm leaving! Rommel, come on!"

Rommel shoved through, as Sandy, seeing him coming,

ducked back into the parlor car once more and wondered why she had even gotten up in the morning, much less come aboard this nightmare train from hell.

Chuck cut to his left, making for the end of the car. As he did so, Rommel's voice sounded in his head. *Did you get him?*

"I've got him on the run."

Seems like we're the ones doing all the running.

Chuck got to the end of the car, threw open the doorway, and stepped into the middle of the short connecting corridor that was between the cars. He heard a scream in the car ahead of him, threw open the connecting door and kept on going.

But then he could go no farther. A crush of people were trying to run in his direction, and he was absolutely blocked in. He couldn't even shove them out of the way with his TK power because they were packed so densely that there was nowhere to shove them to.

"A monster!" someone was screaming. "A monster!"

Chuck immediately realized what had happened. Stalker had smashed through a window farther up ahead, and his entrance had engendered the same sort of warm feelings as had his appearance mere minutes before. God only knew how many people were lying dead up ahead. Indeed, God only knew why such a creature as Stalker had been allowed to exist. And it would have been nice if, just for once, God had elected to let poor, beleaguered Chuck Simon in on what the general plan was.

Chuck and Rommel stepped back into the connecting corridor, which was somewhat wider than the aisle they'd been standing in. The terrified passengers shoved past, and Chuck and Rommel flattened on opposite sides, waiting for the crush to pass. The moment it did, they darted into the car and went up the aisles.

"Where is he?" demanded Chuck. "Rommel—"

I'm not sure. He's not doing anything violent at the moment. That's when I have the best sense of him.

"What, are you telling me I have to wait until he kills some other poor devil so you can lock onto him!" The pain in his arm had faded to a dull ache, but it wasn't making him feel any better.

Don't blame me.

Chuck went quickly up the middle of the train, glancing right and left. Then he stopped at one. There was an elderly dead man in his seventies lying with his hand outstretched toward the door, blood still pooling under his chest.

I think he was here. But he's not anymore. If I get close enough I'll know it's him, but he's not in this car. I'm sure of it.

Chuck didn't even respond. Instead he moved on to the next car, Rommel right behind him.

In this car, a few people were looking out of their parlors in mild confusion. They knew there had been some sort of ruckus, and fellow passengers had even gone running by, shouting in fear. They were asking each other confused questions, and the inclination toward panic was starting to build slowly.

Chuck quickly put up his hands. "Excuse me! Has anyone seen—"

A monster run by here?

"—a monster run . . ." His voice trailed off as the steady babbling immediately increased in volume to barely controlled hysteria. He shot an angry look at Rommel for having put the thought into his mind at a moment when he didn't have the chance to think it through. "—a monstrously large individual run past here," he amended within a second, which wasn't all that much better but at least downplayed an angle bordering on the supernatural.

There were responses of confused and frightened "No's," and Chuck and Rommel kept on moving.

Toward the far end of the car they found an empty parlor and a broken window. Chuck immediately slid the door open and walked in, glancing around. Then he bent down toward the carpet and found a small mass of the decaying stuff that served as Stalker's skin. It had adhered to the carpeting.

"He was in here, all right. Smashed out that window."

How do you know he didn't smash in through the window?

"Because then there would be a lot of glass on the floor, but there's not. So he obviously smashed it outward. Just as obviously, he doubled back . . . or perhaps even went ahead. There's no way we can possibly be sure until we do a car-by-car search and track him down. Here," and he held the small amount of glop between his fingers up to Rommel's nose. "Smell this. Get his scent."

You obviously have me confused with a bloodhound, Rommel remarked snidely. *Do I look like a bloodhound?*

"You've got a nose. Smell."

You've got a nose, too. You smell.

"Rommel, I'm warning you—"

For that matter, you've got a tongue and genitals. Go lick yourself.

"Blast it, Rommel, he's getting away!"

Where are you planning to track him? The great North Woods? I can sense him. I don't have to scent him.

Despite his ire, Chuck was coming to the rapid realization that the dog was correct. They were, after all, in the narrow confines of a train. The only place where Stalker could go was either forward or back, although it was possible that he might continue to scuttle around on the outside of the train. Chuck hoped he wouldn't. He didn't think Stalker would if he didn't absolutely have to, because it was far too easy to let your attention wander and meet a very quick, sudden and grisly death.

And since Stalker's directions were limited, it actually shouldn't be all that difficult. All Chuck had to do was make his way to the front of the train, turn around, and walk the length of it, Rommel psychically scanning every individual they encountered. Sooner or later they'd locate Stalker.

Even as Chuck and Rommel headed for the front, Chuck was wondering why that situation should be. What was it in Stalker's makeup that enabled him to screen his presence from man, but not from animal.

It was, Chuck decided, a highly selective and acquired ability. Stalker's entire forte, clearly, was getting into and out of situations quickly, mercilessly, and hopefully drawing no attention to himself as he would pass by departing the scene of a crime. Of course, under most circumstances, he wasn't encountering a formidable opponent such as Chuck Simon.

Except at the moment, Chuck wasn't feeling very formidable. He was not, in fact, feeling very much like himself at all.

He was a Quaker, blast it. He embraced and celebrated a philosophy and belief that preached tolerance and peace above all. Well, tolerance was a tough call—and being peaceful? He had been attacked again and again, with increasing force. It seemed as if brutality followed him around into every possible circumstance. Followed him with increasing capacity for destruction.

To master aikido and its philosophies was to be able to deflect force, to turn it against itself. To master telekinesis meant that force was able to be kept beyond arm's length. He had thought that that would be enough so that violence would never have to touch him directly.

But it had, with a vengeance. The most recent and horrible was when he had been forced to shoot down Matthew Olivetti, and then psychically smash him apart, rather than let a city of millions suffer at the crazed teen's hands. He had thought that that was going to be the lowest he would ever have to sink, the most blood that would ever be on his hands.

And now it turned out that he was wrong? Was that it? Was he going to have to kill Stalker as well?

If anything, Stalker was worse than the Chaos Kid. The Kid was just confused and angry. Stalker was a malicious, driven bastard. Stalker was more animal than human . . . and that was why, in the final analysis, Rommel was able to get the feeling of him, whereas Chuck could not.

Sensing the thoughts of the human, Rommel thought sanguinely, *Don't worry. I'll kill him for you.* Chuck did not find that suggestion to be remotely comforting.

They reached the front of the train, coming to a halt in front of the door that informed them there was no admittance. He glanced at Rommel and said, "Feel ahead of us. Is he there?"

No. But death is in the air. Someone died right nearby here, through that door. Should we check?

Chuck really didn't feel like looking at yet another corpse. He had already had more than his fill, and had the distinct feeling that there were going to be more. "You're positive he's not up ahead?"

I'd stake your life on it.

"My life?"

I have my limits.

It was good enough for Chuck. He turned and started back down the length of the train, Rommel directly in front of him.

Rommel's great head would swerve from right to left,

like a radar dish. Chuck stayed tight behind him, trying to put aside all of his self-doubts and concerns. What he had to do now was concentrate entirely on the matter at hand. Concentrating on finding and corraling Stalker, before he killed again.

10

"PUT THAT THING away!" snapped Anna.

In their parlor, Jerry Ryder angrily shoved the pistol into his shoulder holster. "There. Are you happy?"

"I'll be happy," she said, "when you stop picking on poor Charlie."

"Poor Charlie might still be a murderer," Ike Stern pointed out from the bench, but he sounded dubious.

She whirled on him. "Oh, great! Now you sound like Jerry!"

"You mean he's just refusing to rule out a still-distinct possibility, that's all."

"What more proof do you need!" said Anna, standing in front of Ryder waving her arms about impatiently. "You talked to that woman. That poor, hysterical woman from the parlor. She saw the two of them together. She saw Chuck and that . . . thing you called Stalker wrestling around on her bed!"

"She thought she saw them. There was a hell of a lot going on, and she might have gotten mixed up . . ."

"Oh, come on, Jerry. You can't be serious. And what

about some of the other people you talked to. The ones who said they saw what looked like a monster coming out of the woman's parlor, and a few seconds later, Charlie came out after it—"

"Look, what counts is what I see with my own two eyes. And I didn't see any monster which might or might not be Stalker. And I didn't see Simon with the monster. All of this is hearsay, and you don't just assume someone is innocent because of hearsay."

"Once upon a time," said Anna stiffly, "you assumed they were innocent because that's the way things were done in this country. Now no one assumes anything except the worst."

"Anna . . ."

He had reached out to put a comforting hand on her arm, but she shook it off angrily. "Don't you 'Anna' me and don't you patronize me. Why don't we really admit what's at stake here. You're determined to try and tag Charlie in some way, shape or form with any or all of the things that have gone on because of the history he and I have. You're jealous."

"Jealous? Oh, honestly—"

"Yes! Honestly! You're jealous of him, and frankly, Jerry, I'm surprised at you. I'd thought better of you than that. I thought you'd be above having that sort of attitude."

"What sort of attitude? The kind that says you—"

At that moment the door slid open and Frank Bamberger was standing there. He looked amazingly composed, considering all that was going on.

Secretly grateful for the chance to break off the conversation which was, as far as he was concerned, going nowhere fast, Ryder called out, "Frank! Great! Get your butt in here! Where's Joe?"

"He'll be along in a few minutes." Frank entered, sliding

the door shut behind himself as Ryder continued. "He just wanted to stop by his room. We checked the length of the train. Didn't find anything unusual."

"At least we can start acting like some sort of an intelligence unit rather than a bunch of bickering kids," and he shot a look at Anna before he continued. "Now look, Ike . . . what did the conductor say when you spoke to him about the dog. About Simon using the creature to 'sniff out' the alleged Stalker."

Anna made a disgusted noise. " 'Alleged' " she muttered, shaking her head at the obtuseness of men.

Ike glanced at her but continued, "He said whatever we thought was best was okay by him."

"Okay. It's nice to know that *someone* trusts us," he said pointedly. "Problem is, Ike, your conversation with the engineer is slightly moot. The animal broke out."

"Jesus," breathed Stern. "Where is it now? Why are we standing around?"

"It's with Simon, sniffing around at the various passengers on this train, in search of Stalker. Anna is under the impression that that's okay and we should trust Simon to do the job for us."

"With all due respect, Anna," said Frank coolly, "this is a job best left to professionals, don't you think? Me, I wouldn't trust Simon farther than I could throw him. I think the guy's crazy myself. He's unpredictable."

"Oh, Frank, not you, too," she sighed.

"People like that, Anna, can turn very quickly. Turn on you or me or Jerry or anyone," Frank told her. He shook his head sadly. "What's the pity is that people don't realize it, and that's understandable. Someone like Simon can have a great deal of personal charm and be very disarming. You don't realize just how dangerous they are until the last moment. By that point, of course, it's much too late."

"So what are you saying, that we should just shoot him down on suspicion?" demanded Anna. "Is that what you're saying, Frank?"

"I'm just saying we should keep our options open. That's all. No more, no less."

"Well, I think it stinks."

"The world stinks, Anna," he said. "We didn't make it that way. But we have to live in it."

"So here's what we do," said Ryder. "We find Simon and his dog, and for the time being, we give them the benefit of the doubt. We assume that the story is true and that Stalker is somewhere on this train and that, presuming Stalker is here, Simon isn't him. We'll stick with Simon and his animal while they try and track him down. And if he makes the slightest wrong move, we take action."

"And what action might that be?" asked Anna stiffly.

He barely glanced at her. "Whatever action is required. No more and no less than that."

"You know," Bamberger said darkly, "there's something about that guy, I'm telling you. Something that I can't put my finger on. I swear, he's more than he appears."

"Oh, nonsense," said Anna.

And it was at that moment that the door to their parlor car slid open, and the moment after that that all hell broke loose.

Chuck and Rommel had made their way over half the length of the train, and Chuck was just beginning to get nervous. What if they didn't find him? What if they went the full distance of the train, wound up all the way back in baggage again, and Stalker still had not been found? Then did they start back in the other direction again?

As they would pass by compartments, glancing in through the large, tight curtains that were drawn across the parlor car windows facing out into the corridor, every so often someone would peer out at them fearfully. And sometimes those eyes would widen in recognition and withdraw quickly into the parlor. He would even, on occasion, hear a terrified shriek as he went past. Apparently, he realized, a number of people on the train were still going on the belief that he was the murderous monster stalking the Bullet Train.

He remembered once hearing an old expression: You couldn't tell the good guys from the bad guys without a program. That certainly was applicable now.

He stopped in briefly at his own compartment to see how things were going. To his surprise, not only was Sandy there, but also the woman whom he had saved shortly before. She had taken the time to pull some clothes on, and she was sitting next to Sandy now, curled up in a fetal position. Her eyes were dark and wide and turned inward, as if afraid to look out into the real world.

Sandy looked up at Chuck and said softly, "She didn't want to stay in her own parlor."

"Understandable," said Chuck.

"Besides," continued Sandy, "the head conductor sealed it off. Didn't want anyone going in there."

"No one would want to."

"Are you kidding?" Her face wrinkled in disgust. "People were crowding in trying to get a peek at what happened. I swear humans are a morbid bunch."

The woman seated next to Sandy slowly looked up at Chuck, her eyes seeming to focus for the first time. She said nothing, but it was immediately clear to Chuck that she recognized him as the man who had saved her earlier. Very slowly, one time, her head went up and down in a prolonged nod of acknowledgement.

He forced a smile. It was difficult, considering the distant and battered manner of the woman. But he did it. Then he withdrew from the parlor and continued down the corridor.

What's her problem?

"She saw either her boyfriend or husband torn apart by the monster we're after."

What did she do about it?

"There was nothing she could do."

Rommel sniffed disdainfully. *Humans. Amazing that they think they're in charge of the world.*

"Well, we like to kid ourselves. But there are many people who say that, sooner or later, the entire planet is going to go to the dogs."

Well that certainly makes sense.

"Yes, I thought you'd be pleased."

Not that you're leaving it in any great shape for us.

"Sorry. We're doing our best."

Yes, you've already made clear what humans doing their best entails.

They moved farther down the corridor, into the next car, and suddenly Rommel became alert. His tail stuck straight out behind him, and he growled, *He's here. Right there. Up ahead. I have him.*

"Where?" Chuck's voice was now filled with urgency. "Is he hurting anyone?"

Not yet. Let's get him. It's that one right there, and he indicated the parlor ahead with a wave of his muzzle.

Alarm immediately slammed through Chuck, because he recognized the parlor immediately. It was the one that Anna was staying in with that fool of a fiancé.

Then he saw, coming from the other direction, the young conductor. He was stammering, something about the gym and a body, and Chuck shouted, "Stay back!" The conductor froze in his tracks, and Chuck now moved like lightning, worried that his bellow might have alerted Stalker to his presence.

He yanked the door open and froze in the doorframe.

Anna turned to look at him, her face a question, and Ryder now spotted him as well. Two other men were in the room, the one called Bamberger and the one called Stern.

Just behind him Rommel practically snarled in his head, *That one! The taller one! That's him!*

"Are you sure!" demanded Chuck.

"Yes! Yes! And he's going to kill the woman!"

And sure enough, Frank Bamberger, standing just behind Anna, was looking straight at Chuck with the malevolent eyes of Stalker as he stepped toward Anna. She hadn't noticed; none of them had, for they were looking at Chuck and his frenzied expression.

What Chuck did next he did without thinking, motivated entirely by frantic fear that the creature was going to tear Anna to shreds before his very eyes.

His TK power struck, and he lifted the man with Bamberger's face clear off the floor. Bamberger's arms and legs were spread wide, a scream torn from his throat, as Chuck crushed him against the far wall with such force that he nearly killed him then and there. It was a massive effort of will that, at the last moment, he held off and merely pinned him with formidable force.

"He's gone *crazy*!" shouted Bamberger. "I knew it! I warned you! I knew there was something about him!"

"Stop it!" Chuck said fiercely. "It's over! I'll kill you if I have to, if that's the only way to stop you from hurting her, but it's over!" And behind him, Rommel howled a challenge, shoving his way into the room.

And the gun roared in the enclosure of the room.

Ryder's eyes opened wide as he saw what was happening before him, even as Ike Stern was shouting, "I don't believe it! I don't believe it!" Anna was making a bizarre, terrified keening noise. He couldn't blame them. He could barely believe it himself.

With absolutely no outside force, Chuck Simon had lifted Frank Bamberger clear off the ground. Ryder had gathered the information, studied the confidential reports, knew intellectually what was happening in the world, and yet now, confronted with evidence of it before his very eyes, he was still thunderstruck at the sheer insanity of it all.

And that was when the tumblers of his mind clicked in. Simon the telekinetic. Psi-Man the telekinetic.

Simon. Psi-Man.

My God, he had been completely blind.

The renegade, berserk psionic had literally been under their very noses, and he hadn't realized it.

The rest of it came clear to him in an eyeblink. Stalker wasn't on the train. Stalker was dead. It had all been a red herring. It was Simon, Simon all along. The Psi-Man had found out somehow that SPEAR was being reorganized and had obviously taken their threat seriously. But he had gambled that his past affiliation with Ryder's fiancée would give him a measure of safe conduct, and to a degree he had been right. Always Anna had spoken up for him. Always Anna had blocked Ryder's vision of what was the true and sensible path.

Psi-Man had been trying to pick them off one by one. That was it. He had killed Rita, and Al had to be dead as well. Thank God Joe and Frank hadn't run into him alone, or they'd be dead by now as well. Maybe he even figured that there would be a bonus tossed in. That when he knocked off all of them, including Ryder, he could then get Anna back. Why not? Helpless. Defenseless. She would be a prime candidate for his nefarious ends.

But Frank had tumbled to him. Frank was already voicing

his suspicions, and probably suspected even more than he had been saying. Frank always had been a bit tight-lipped.

Afraid of being found out, Psi-Man had panicked. He had tossed aside all caution and was now hoping to make a fast, preemptive strike, taking them out, powered by the element of surprise. And with his formidable power and that monstrous dog of his backing him up, he just might have pulled it off.

He had not, however, banked on the reflexes of Jerome Ryder. For in addition to being one of the best information-gatherers in the business, Ryder was also a crack shot.

The gun was already in his hand, and he brought it around, aimed in one movement squarely into the middle of Psi-Man's head, and started to squeeze the trigger.

It was Anna who spotted it, snapping from her paralysis and leaping forward with a scream of alarm. She smashed his arm upward, partially ruining his aim.

But only partially.

The bullet exploded from the muzzle, and Chuck's head snapped back. Blood spurted from his forehead, and Chuck's eyes rolled up in the back of his head. He grunted and tumbled backward, falling like a tree.

The monstrous German shepherd yelped in alarm, his entrance partially blocked by the fallen body of his master. The canine backpedaled, and Frank Bamberger fell to the ground, the psionic hold no longer in place.

The dog wheeled to face the new threat, his muzzle drawn back exposing a double row of teeth that could have ripped Ryder's arm off at the elbow.

Anna was screaming his name, pounding on his back, and Ike had recovered from his shock enough to hold Anna back. Ryder swung his gun around, aimed at the dog, and fired point-blank.

The dog yelped as fur flew, the bullet passing cleanly

through his right flank. Filled with consternation and confusion, barking loudly and in fury at Psi-Man's unmoving body, the dog backed up. He swung his head and just barely avoided a second bullet that winged past him and almost clipped his ear.

Infuriated that he had to retreat, Rommel still saw no choice. His massive body withdrew from the parlor, and the door rolled shut, intercepting another bullet that would have taken him square between the eyes. He turned and ran for the far end of the car, and there he came to a halt. The door was closed at the far end, and Rommel couldn't operate the hand or foot devices to get it to open. He was trapped there, and his only hope was that the crazy gunman wasn't going to come after him, because if he did then Rommel was dead.

Fortunately for Rommel, but unfortunately for the gunman, it became a moot question within a very few minutes.

"It's a mistake!" Anna was wailing. "It's a mistake! It has to be a mistake!"

"It's no mistake!" shouted Ryder. "Goddammit, Anna, open your eyes! Look at what he did! Look at what he was capable of! It was him! Him all along!"

Chuck lay on the floor, unmoving. The front of his face was now covered with blood and it was staining the floor. Anna dropped to the ground next to him, ripping off a piece of her sleeve and desperately trying to staunch the bleeding. "It wasn't! He's the sweetest, kindest man I ever met! He would never do what you're accusing him of!"

"Sweet?!" demanded Ryder.

"Yes!"

"Kind?!"

"Yes!"

"And could he lift a man off his feet just through the

power of his mind! Could he do that? Was that one of the sweet, kind things he used to do when you were married! Look at him, Anna! He's a mad-dog killer! That's all he ever was!"

"Stop it!" she shrieked. "Stop it! Stop saying these things!" She put a hand against Chuck's face, her palm coming away dark red. "We have to help him!"

"Help him? He's going to die!" said Ryder triumphantly. "We brought him down! Us! SPEAR! We're together again, and we nailed Rita and Al's killer!"

He stuck out a hand, palm down, in front of Stern. Stern, not quite as enthused as Ryder but smiling gamely, put out his hand and slapped it down on top of Ryder's, a gesture of unity and solidarity.

And Bamberger's hand followed.

But it went through Stern first.

It went through his back and exploded out through Stern's stomach, a gory, red, taloned *thing* that extended from out of Stern's stomach and clapped down on the hands of the other two men.

Stern, not yet realizing he was dead, looked down at the arm in amazement, watched his vitals gathering around it and dripping to the floor. Anna screamed, the scream getting louder and louder and filling up everything, reaching a high-pitched keening whine that was just everywhere.

The front of Ryder's shirt and trousers was covered with the blood of Stern, and he couldn't believe it, just couldn't goddamn *believe* it, as Bamberger lifted his arm up, still transfixing Stern's body. And Stern was still *alive*, he was *alive*, somehow still not getting the idea that he didn't have a prayer.

Stern rose up, and his head was crushed against the roof of the parlor with a sound like an overripe melon splitting. Behind him the creature that pretended to be Bamberger was roaring with laughter, and he snarled, "You are just so fucking stupid, Jerry. You know that? I was going to let you live a while longer, but you are just too stupid to live."

He lowered his arm and Stern, lifeless, slid off it, landing on the floor across Chuck's legs.

Ryder started to bring his gun up, but Stalker had already reached out and grabbed Anna's arm. He yanked her in front of him and whispered, "Go ahead, Jerry. Go right ahead. Pump your lovely fiancée full of great big holes." She struggled in his grasp but couldn't make the slightest bit of headway.

"Let her go, Stalker," said Ryder, astounded that his voice was as calm as it was. Deathly calm. "This isn't her fight. This has nothing to do with her."

"But it has to do with you, and so it has to do with her," said Stalker. His conversational tone was a horrifying contrast to the thick, red gore that covered his arms. "First thing is, Jerry old pal, you drop the gun. Right now." And when Ryder hesitated, Stalker clamped his hands around her throat. He squeezed ever so gently, and Anna gagged, her eyes bulging out. "Right . . . now," Stalker repeated, with the air of someone who was on the verge of losing his temper.

"All right!" Ryder said quickly, and he dropped the firearm. "All right! See? See there? I put it down."

"Yes, I see you put it down. That was very good of you. You're a smart man, Jerry. The only dumb thing you ever did was when you set me up."

"We never set you up, Stalker," Ryder began.

Stalker's taloned fingers, which had loosened slightly in their grip on Anna's throat, now closed tightly again. His face was flowing, rivulets of flesh streaming about with lives of their own. It was re-forming into something that was a grotesque mockery of a man's face. The brow was

thick and distended, barbaric-looking, causing the eyes to
be inset so deep that they became merely two blackened
pools of hatred. Eerily, even his hair changed color, going
from gray to a firey red, and then was gone completely, as
if it had burned completely off his head. His nose was
withdrawn so far into his face that it was little more than a
skeletal socket.

"I'm sorry," said Stalker calmly, "I thought you were
trying to lie to me. I can't stand when people try to lie."

"It's no lie! We didn't . . . !"

Thin droplets of blood were now running down Anna's
perfect throat—her blood from the holes Stalker was drilling in her with his newly formed claws.

"All right! All right!" howled Ryder. "I'll say whatever
you want me to say! You want me to tell you you were set
up? Fine! Fine! You were set up!"

"I don't want to hear just anything, Jer," said Stalker
calmly. "I want you to tell me just how much you enjoyed
setting me up and ditching me."

"I didn't enjoy it!" Ryder started to take a step toward
him and then thought better of it and stayed where he was.
"It was the toughest thing I ever did! They were terrified of
you, Stalker. Everybody was!"

"Who blew the building?"

"Stern."

"You're saying that because he's dead."

Ryder felt swept up by the madness of it all. "Well you
killed just about everybody! The odds were pretty damned
good you killed the one who blew the building, now, aren't
they! Stern was the munitions expert!"

"So the mission was—?"

Ryder sighed, a deep, trembling thing in his chest. "We
were to go deep into enemy territory. Supposedly there was
a group of raiders hidden in that plant. Only we were to

make sure that when the plant was blown, you were still in there."

"That's why you pretended that Rita was still in there," said Stalker. "You sent me back in to get her, the next thing I knew there's an explosion, the place was collapsing around my ears, and who-knows-how-long later, the enemy was pulling me from under the rubble, scraping me out with a spoon."

"Rita was hiding safely outside of the building. She had her orders. We all had our orders, Stalker, I swear to God—"

"Oh, you can swear to God all you want," said Stalker with incredible calmness. "And it's going to do you jack-shit. Do you have any idea what my life was like after that? Do you? I'll tell you. They were fascinated by my skin. By my strength. By everything I could do. So they kept me in a lab, under lock and key, drugged and doped and unable to think or feel anything. And they poked and prodded, month after month, year after year. They kept taking pieces of my skin. Tried cloning me. Tried making other people like me. You should have seen the roomful of volunteers, howling and screeching after they'd been injected with my DNA. Watching their skin melt and burn off them and leaving them just skeletons. Grinning, leering skeletons."

"Stalker, please—" Ryder started desperately.

Stalker didn't even seem to hear him. "They had no idea, of course. No idea what they were dealing with. No idea that eventually I would build up immunities to their little drugs. And one night . . . one night, I destroyed them all, Jerry. Shame you weren't there. It was a slaughter, just an incredible slaughter. Because you see, up until then, I hadn't developed the ability to sharpen up my skin the way that I have now. It's just something that I started to acquire the knack for while I was in their hands. Pretty effective, don't you think?"

This time Ryder didn't respond, nor did there seem to be any point in doing so. "I slit dozens of throats that night," said Stalker. "It was a sea of blood, just pouring everywhere. And I got away, and started the long trip back. Of course, by the time I got back here, years had passed. Good old SPEAR had broken up. Outmoded, outdated. Except you weren't, were you. The government saw possibilities for you in this Psi-Man business, didn't they? Decided to bring you back together by popular demand. You were one popular bunch of guys, you know that?" He shook his head. "So when I found out that you folks were going to be getting together for this little government-sponsored reunion, I just couldn't stay away. I hope you understand."

His fingers had eased up on the throat of the petrified Anna once more, but there were still trickles of blood down her. She was trembling, her face deathly white, and Stalker said, "Imagine, though. Bagging not only you guys, but the Psi-Man fellow that you were supposed to be going after. It's truly a small world, wouldn't you say? Well, now, Jerry . . . here's the gag," and his voice abruptly switched tone, sounding wheedling. "I'm going to give you a choice. Now before you get your hopes up," he said consolingly, "I have to warn you, either way, you die. I mean, you do understand that. It's the principle of the thing.

"Anyway—your little lady here is really adorable. Even better than Rita. So . . . either I can kill her now, and then you. Or," and he raised his voice slightly, because Anna had gasped and started making little noises of panic, and he had to talk over them. "Or, or, or," he continued, "here's the other possibility. I rape her and make you watch. Then I'll kill you . . . but I'll let her live. So you're determining her future here. Think carefully, but think quickly. I mean, you haven't got very much time. Not much time at all."

Ryder's eyes flickered desperately to Anna's, and he found that he couldn't even look at her directly. There was such terror, such desperation, and he couldn't do anything, dammit, anything.

"Decide, Jer. Now," said Stalker. "Or I decide for you. And you never know what I'll decide. I mean, some people say I'm actually unstable."

And that was when Ike Stern got to his feet, dead eyes staring out at the world, and lurched at Stalker.

11

THE APPARITION CAUGHT Stalker completely off guard.

He let out a gasp of amazement as the dead man reared up in front of him, shoulders heaving back, looking like the reincarnation of Dr. Frankenstein's monster. "What the *hell!*" shouted Stalker, and then Ike was upon him.

Totally unnerved, Stalker reacted on impulse and shoved Anna directly at him. With a shriek she slammed into him, and the two of them went down in a tangle of live limbs with dead ones.

Seeing Stalker unprotected, Ryder immediately lunged for his gun. But he was far too slow, and Stalker grabbed Ryder's wrist, turned and smashed his head into the wall. Ryder groaned and fell to the parlor bench, Stalker turning on him, his hand drawn back in to his razor fist to finish the job.

And that was when an invisible smash crashed against his chest, sending him staggering back and reeling into the door.

Chuck Simon rose as from the dead. His face was blood

red, his breath rattling in his chest, but his eyes were afire with fury.

Then Chuck sagged, momentary weakness overcoming him. And Stalker, seizing the opportunity, yanked open the door, leaped into the train corridor, and slammed the door shut behind him.

At the far end of the corridor, Rommel saw him. With a roar, the giant dog charged, his massive feet thudding on the carpeted floor like a fusillade of cannon fire.

Stalker saw those huge teeth and somehow didn't want to try and match his shape-changing abilities against them. He turned and ran.

Rommel was right behind him, snarling, and Stalker got to the door that separated them from the next car. He threw it open, but just as he started to pass through, Rommel sank his teeth into Stalker's rear leg. The immense jaws clamped down through to the bone, and Stalker howled at the grip, trying to yank his leg clear. Rommel would have none of it, growling fiercely and shaking his head as if he were worrying a soup bone.

Huge gobs of Stalker's malleable skin tore away, left behind in Rommel's jaw, and Stalker stumbled forward into the connecting corridor. The door rolled shut, catching Rommel's muzzle. With a yelp of anger and annoyance, Rommel withdrew, and the door slammed shut, separating them.

Rommel roared and hurled himself against the door, all in great futility. No matter how much he pounded against it, it wouldn't give.

Stalker pulled open the door and came face to hideous face with trainee conductor Richard Goldstein.

Richard took one look at him and fainted dead away.

Stalker stepped over his body and kept on going, mind racing. This whole business was starting to wear thin for him. He was going to have to end it sooner or later, and it was best if it was sooner.

With a fierce limp, he started up the corridor. Then his leg weakened, and he thudded against one of the parlor doors.

He braced himself and the door opened. He heard a female voice call out, "Simon?" and then he caught a glimpse of two women, one of whom he recognized immediately. The woman he didn't recognize gasped, and the woman whom he did know—the woman whose husband or boyfriend or whatever he had left gutted on the floor of their compartment—shrieked when she saw him.

The parlor door slammed in his face, and he momentarily toyed with the thought of forcing his way in there and giving the two of them what they doubtlessly had coming. But he had bigger problems to attend to—

Like wrecking the train, for example.

"We don't have time for this!" said Chuck impatiently.

"We make the time," said Anna firmly. She had cleaned away all the blood and was now bandaging the wound in his forehead. "The blood made it look a lot worse than it was. I think the bullet just creased your skull."

"Oh good, at least nothing important was put at risk," said Chuck. "I still think I hear a ringing in my head."

"That will pass," said Ryder, looking embarrassed and chagrined. "Look, Simon . . . I mean, I was wrong, okay? About you. Not about everything about you—you still got that power, I was right about that."

"Yes, that power, Charlie," Anna looked at him with a sense of wonder. "How on earth—"

"I don't understand it myself," said Chuck. "It's the biggest blessing and curse in my life, and I would give anything to be rid of it. But that's not going to happen anytime soon, so I just live with it. Sometimes I make overt use of it, and sometimes I'm subtle."

"What would you call," asked Ryder, looking down with a shudder at Ike's unmoving body, "using it to animate a corpse? Make it look like someone had risen from the dead?"

"I'd call that inspired," said Chuck. He got to his feet and then steadied himself briefly as the world seemed to swirl around him for a moment before coming to a halt. He let out a breath in relief and then went out the door.

Rommel was standing there waiting for him. "Which way?" he demanded. Rommel pointed with his muzzle and replied, *That way.*

"Charlie, what do we do?" asked Anna.

"You stay here," began Ryder.

But Chuck turned toward them quickly. "The hell she does. We stay together. Haven't you ever seen a horror movie, Ryder? When the people split up, they get picked off one at a time. That's what's been happening to you and your people. If we're all together—"

"Then he can kill us in one shot," said Ryder.

"It's the only way and the sensible way. Now come on."

Led by Rommel at point, Chuck, Ryder, and Anna started forward.

They moved quickly, efficiently, going back in the direction they had come earlier, and Rommel slowed down every several feet to make sure that he wasn't getting a sense of the animalistic Stalker. Chuck allowed himself a brief flash of amazement. Rommel was really doing a top-notch job here.

Several people were emerging from their parlors, looking around and asking each other if they had heard the latest and what the hell was happening. They afforded Chuck nervous glances, and became even more nervous when they realized just how big his canine companion was.

And that was when the train suddenly lurched.

It staggered them a moment, then they pulled themselves up, looking at each other in confusion. "What caused that?" demanded Ryder. Anna looked around worriedly.

"I'm not sure," said Chuck, "but I'll tell you what. I got this feeling that the train is moving faster than it has been."

"How'd he manage that?"

"I'm not sure I want to know, but I am sure that we'd better find out. Come on."

They made their way through the cars as quickly as they could, and when they got to the one that was second from the front, they ran straight into head engineer Adam Thaler. Chuck slowed down his pace as the heavier, older man came toward them, and he tossed a glance at Rommel. Rommel didn't react at all—it was evident that the approaching man was not Stalker in yet another disguise.

Thaler regarded him with suspicion, although clearly he was willing to accept the evidence of Thaler's approval by dint of his standing next to the supposed murderer. Trying to get past this opening gambit of clear suspicion, Chuck said, "Is it my imagination, or has the train—?"

"Picked up speed, yes," said Thaler worriedly. "We were due into New York in just over an hour. I'm not sure how fast we're moving at this point, but it's got to be at least 250. Maybe even faster."

Chuck glanced at Ryder. "Stalker?"

"Got to be," said Ryder.

The train shuddered again, and the people in the hallway felt the subtle shift of pressure. "How fast can this thing go?" asked Chuck.

"Cruising speed is 200. If we go much above 300, or even maintain it for any period of time, we can go hurtling off the track. We're not designed to maintain magnetic adherence at these kinds of speeds. Besides, if we can't brake the damned thing, we won't be able to stop once we get to the other end. We'll go straight through and smash to pieces against the terminal. It'll be a spectacular wreck. Too bad that none of us will be alive to see it."

"Terrific. And how is this happening?"

"Our friend must be in the command cab."

"Have you gone in to check?"

Thaler looked at Ryder in disbelief. "Yeah. Right."

"Okay, come on."

The ragtag band headed for the command cab, and moments later were standing directly outside. Chuck pulled experimentally on the handle, and wasn't surprised to find it didn't budge. His TK power enabled him to reach in and open some types of locks, but this wasn't one of them.

Rommel growled. *He's in there.*

"What's with him?" asked Thaler, pointing nervously at the dog.

"He says that Stalker is in there."

"Well I'm certainly not going to be the one to disagree with him," said Thaler. He pulled out his pass card. "I can get you in. You'll excuse me if I don't follow you."

"Understood," said Chuck. He put his hand against the door pull, ready to yank it open.

And Ryder said, "Simon . . . I should go in first. I'm the trained agent. He killed my friends. I should take the point."

Chuck looked at him for a long moment and then said, "You have a future planned. A future with a wonderful woman who deserves one. I'm day to day. That's how it'll be until the last day. Now just back me up, okay."

He turned back to the door and nodded for the conductor

to run his pass card through the receptacle. As Thaler did
so, Ryder said, "Simon."

"*Now* what?"

"Just want you to know I'm sorry about shooting you."

"Don't worry," said Chuck evenly. "If I can ever do the
same for you, I will."

He closed his eyes, breathed in and out quickly, and then
yanked open the door and charged in.

There was no one in the command cab.

He took a few steps toward the computer array that
blinked steadily at the front of the train, and then turned and
started to call out to the people behind him.

And just as he turned, the door of the private bathroom
slammed outward, ripped right out of its fixtures, and the
slab of metal smashed into him. Chuck staggered back and
fell against the computer console.

Stalker emerged from the bathroom, erupted from the
bathroom, slamming shut the entrance door to the cab
before anyone else could make it in. Then he was across the
enclosed area and leaping at Chuck.

Chuck had been momentarily stunned by the slab of
metal, and then Stalker grabbed Chuck by the chest and
scruff of the neck, swung him up with incredible strength,
and started smashing him headfirst into the windscreen of
the cab.

Chuck heard shouts and yelling and barking from outside, and an angry voice in his head saying, *Would you get
it together please? This is embarrassing!* He wasn't sure if
it was Rommel's voice or if perhaps he was simply chiding
himself.

His head was speeding toward the windscreen once more,
and Chuck, barely thinking, blew out the windscreen with
his TK power so that his head wouldn't hit it. The command
cab filled with the rush of air blasting in at more than 250

miles per hour, and Chuck Simon was shoved out the front window.

He started to tumble off the front of the train, and then the windspeed and his own TK power saved him as he was blown back and crushed against the front of the train, which tapered down like a bullet. He was spread-eagled across the front, pinned there, clutching on for dear life. He didn't need his TK power to anchor him. The wind was so intense that not only was it holding him in place, but it threatened to reduce him to a flesh-colored pulp.

He saw just above him, in the window, the image of Stalker laughing and laughing, and Chuck struck out with his TK power and seized Stalker, dragging him forward as well.

The assassin struggled in the grip of Chuck's mind power, trying to anchor himself, but he couldn't get a hold on anything, and he didn't have the time to return his skin to its adhesive quality. He was yanked straight out on the front of the train, and now the wind crushed him against the curved, cone-shaped nose as well.

They were smeared against the nose of the train, a train that was picking up speed with every passing second. In the darkness that had fallen, the sky hung overhead, and still the gray of the world obscured the stars twinkling down. All was simply blackness.

Stalker was shouting something, but the roar of the wind was carrying it away. His ruined faced was twisted and defiant as he clutched onto the speeding nose of the train, riding the bullet, and Stalker started to crawl toward him, shaping his hands into razor sharpness.

Chuck saw what he meant to do. He meant to slice Chuck's hands off, preferably at the wrist.

Chuck did the only thing he could. He lashed out with his TK power, jamming it under Stalker, and prying. Stalker's face twisted in alarm, and that was all the time that Chuck had to see it before Stalker disappeared, just vanished, whipped away by the high-speed winds. One moment he was there, and the next he was gone, like a magician performing a trick.

Gone. Gone. Stalker was gone. It went through Chuck's mind in a bizarre sing song-type pattern. Chuck refused even to consider for a moment what had happened to his enemy, being hurled off a train moving at the speed they were. Had anything been left after he'd finished rolling? Was his body simply smashed beyond recognition. Or perhaps—horror of horrors—was his brain still functioning in a body smashed beyond ability to function? Perhaps he was lying beside a track, unable to move as his life's blood ebbed from him.

Maliciously, Chuck hoped so.

Then, far ahead, but not too far, he could see the blinking lights of the Manhattan skyline. It reminded him that, within the hour, they were going to reach the literal end of the line.

Bracing himself with his TK power, Chuck inched up the front of the cab. The window was just above him, and now in it he could see the face of the conductor shouting to him. Everyone was always shouting at him. His mind and body were exhausted, and somehow all he wanted to do was just close his eyes, just for a few minutes, get some rest, get some sleep.

And a voice shouted at him angrily, *Don't you dare! Don't you dare! You just get in here! This is no time to take a stupid human being rest, and you just move it, you understand?*

Chuck understood all too clearly. He inched his way up the front of the command cab, the metal cold as ice beneath him. He stretched out his hand as far as he could, and then several hands were reaching through the shattered front, grabbing him and hauling him up into the command cab and safety.

Moments later he was leaning against the computer console, trying to catch his breath, and the engineer and Ryder were both shouting at him, asking about Stalker.

"Gone!" hollered Chuck. "Wind yanked him away!"

"Good riddance!" the conductor shouted back. "Now we just have one problem, namely, that we're all going to get killed in just a few minutes."

"Shut the train down!" Chuck told him.

"We can't! He's done something to the computer, and we have no idea how to override it!"

Chuck, leaning against the computer console, looked down and formed his TK power into a spear. He drove it straight down into the heart of the computer, smashing apart the circuitry, shredding it.

They passed a large, blinking sign overhead, visible for miles ahead, that read TERMINAL AHEAD TEN MILES. SPEED MUST BE REDUCED NOW.

The others in the cab fell back as the train began to lurch wildly, but Chuck held on and continued to pummel the computer with the power of his mind. He gutted the entire display, ripping out whatever he could, smashing the rest.

Not too far ahead of them loomed the terminal, coming up with horrifying speed. Everything was hurtling past at breakneck pace, and there were going to be quite a few broken necks on the train if they didn't manage to stop.

There was an ear-splitting creak of metal as his mind pushed against the top of the console, caving it in. Pieces of metal twisted and bent back on themselves, and relays began to sizzle and burn.

He stepped back, and his TK power ripped out the entire

command unit. Metal hung in the air, crunching in on itself, circuit boards being bent in half or just crushed.

The train lurched once more, and for just a moment Chuck was certain that the entire thing was going to be hurled right off the track, tumbling over and over and crashing and burning.

And then the train began to slow. Imperceptibly at first, and then more and more the speed diminished, dropping below 200 miles per hour and continuing to slow.

And very gradually, and very steadily, the Bullet Train slowed to a crawl and then halted completely.

The men looked at each other in disbelief, their breath ragged in their chests. "We'll reprogram it manually," said Chuck, making a poor attempt at humor.

Ryder pointed out the window, and Chuck looked to where he was indicating. There, not far ahead, was a sign that read WELCOME TO NEW YORK. 1000 FEET TO TERMINAL.

Chuck shrugged. "1000 feet. We had a thousand whole feet left. Heck, that wasn't even close."

12

CHUCK HAD STAGGERED all the way to his parlor, not wanting to talk to anyone. Every part of his body ached, everything seemed covered with bruises. When he'd gotten there, Sandy and the other woman had still been there. He hadn't wanted to see them either, or talk to anyone, or think about anything except just letting utter exhaustion claim him.

It was going to be a little while yet before they were actually in the terminal. With its guidance systems smashed, the train was as good as inoperative. They had to roll a towing car out onto the track and physically drag them into the station. All of that was going to take time, and Chuck wanted to use that time to just try and get some rest.

Out of consideration for that, Sandy and the woman had agreed to move over to one of the unoccupied cabins. However, the woman was so jittery over potentially being attacked again—despite Chuck's assurances to the contrary— that he had sent Rommel along with them to act as bodyguard and insurance of their continued safety.

He lay on the parlor couch, his knifed shoulder still stiff

and aching, his wounded forehead still throbbing. He wanted nothing more than to do nothing.

There was a knock at the door.

"Go away!" he called. "I mean it!"

"Honey?" came a voice.

Anna's voice.

Immediately he sat up. "Anna?"

"Yes. Can I talk to you?"

He wondered what on earth it could be about. Already, deep within his soul, he was praying that he knew. He wanted it so much to be . . .

But she wouldn't . . .

Would she?

"Okay. Okay, come in. It isn't locked."

The door slid open and Anna entered. She had, understandably, changed out of the blood-soaked clothes, and stood poised in the doorframe, as if afraid to come in. "Is it okay?"

"Yeah. Yeah, it's okay," he said slowly. She looked so tentative, as if something of great importance was on her mind.

She walked slowly across the cabin, allowing the door to slide shut behind her. There was a slight hitch in her step, as if she were coming toward him reluctantly but unable to stop herself.

She sat down on the couch next to him.

"I want to come with you," she said.

"What?" He couldn't believe it. "Look . . . Anna . . . I loved being married to you. You know I'd want to again in a minute. But . . . but what about your fiancé . . . ?"

She shook her head "Next to you, he's nothing. I saw how he behaved. I saw how he attacked you. How he didn't believe you. I stuck up for you, but he didn't care what I said. How am I supposed to spend a lifetime with a man who doesn't care what I say? Does that sound reasonable to you?"

"No," he whispered.

She faced him, putting her hands on his shoulders. "I want to stay with you. You're . . . you're everything that I could possibly have wanted. I know that now. Everything. But . . . but when I tell him I'm leaving him, he'll go crazy. You'll protect me, won't you?"

"Of course I will. But . . . But Anna . . ." He couldn't believe it was happening. His heart was singing, and yet it was so unfair not to let her know. "The life I'm leading now—I don't see how you can possibly share it."

"I know I can—"

"It's dangerous. There are people after me . . . you have no idea." He took her hand. She was trembling, her hand cold with fear. Her lower lip was quivering. "People who want to capture me, or kill me. And I'm afraid that they'll do the same to you. If you share that life, you share tremendous danger."

"I don't care. I want to be with you, Chuck. You're the only man I ever truly loved. I see that, now. I was crazy to leave you. It's always been you. Never anyone else."

Her hands were working at the bottom of his shirt, working their way under. He shivered, his blood pounding in him.

She worked his shirt up over his head even as he whispered, "No, this isn't right. I want you back, but . . . it's not fair . . . you deserve a life . . ."

"I deserve a life with you." She tossed his shirt aside and started to kiss his chest. "Please don't make me leave, Chuck. I can make you feel so good . . ."

Her lips moved down the expanse of his stomach, going lower, and her hands were doing things to him, incredible things. The world was starting to haze out around him . . .

And there was a faint buzz . . .

And his name . . .

Chuck.

Twice she'd called him Chuck.

Never.

Always Charlie.

And her hands were cold, like death . . .

With a scream, Chuck sat up and shoved her away just as a taloned hand slashed out. It ripped across the cushion, sending stuffing flying.

Anna got to her feet with preternatural speed and charged at Chuck, who was paralyzed at the image approaching him with death in her eye. His mind just seized up, locked on him, unable to deal with the sudden twist in emotions, unable to believe what had just nearly happened to him.

With a roar Anna came at him, fingers curved into taloned death, and suddenly there was a deafening explosion. Anna shrieked as the front of her chest exploded, the bullet continuing through her and blowing open the window. Chuck hit the floor, staring up at her in horror and disbelief.

Jerome Ryder was in the doorway, gun braced with both hands, and he fired a second time.

The top of Anna's head exploded, and she fell back. She was dead before she hit the ground.

And as she lay there, Chuck's greatest nightmare incarnate, her skin began to lose its cohesion. It shifted around, melting off like a burning candle, dripping on the floor.

And within moments, Stalker was lying on the ground, unmoving.

There were the sounds of racing feet now, people coming from all over having heard the shots. Ryder stood frozen in the doorway, gun at the ready, as if waiting for the immobile thing on the floor to become mobile once more. It didn't, but instead simply lay there, a dark puddle spreading outward on the floor.

"Let me through!" one female voice was rising above the others, and moments later Anna was peering in through the door. She gasped at the sight she beheld.

"I was coming here," said Ryder quietly, "to fill you in on information I'd learned about certain government programs. Programs to create psionic humans. I thought you could use the information. And I wanted to apologize once more. To tell you how much I owed you. But from here, it kind of looks like we're even."

Chuck stared at the corpse on the floor. The skin was continuing to just come right off of the bone, a disgusting mess. He had seen the wind yank the creature away, down the length of the train, but obviously he'd managed to grab a handhold and save himself.

If he'd just stayed in hiding, or even just hopped off when the train had halted, he would have gotten away. Clean away.

"He wanted more blood," said Chuck incredulously. "All the blood on his hands, and he wanted more!"

Ryder stared down at him. "There isn't that much blood in the whole world."

13

ANNA BROWN AND Jerome Ryder walked through the terminal together, each wrapped in their own thoughts. All around them people were running about, trying to discover what had happened. Word had spread throughout the place of all kinds of terrible doings on the Bullet Train, and morbid speculation was running rampant. Of course, the speculation couldn't hold a candle to what had really happened.

And then Chuck and Rommel stepped out in front of them, almost as if materializing from the shadows.

They stopped and stared at one another for a long moment. "The authorities want to talk to you," said Ryder quietly.

Chuck, wearing dark glasses, a newly purchased cap pulled low to cover the bandage on his forehead, said, "Authorities always want to talk to me. I'm a very popular guy."

"You're not planning on it?"

"No. No plans. You going to try and make me?"

Ryder appeared to consider the idea, and then dismissed it. "Nah. Besides, what would you tell them? The truth? The last thing they'd want to hear is that."

"It's too disgusting," agreed Chuck.

You want her. Let's take her and be done with it. Rommel said.

"No," said Chuck quietly.

"No what?" asked Ryder.

"Do you mind if I speak with Charlie for a moment?" Anna said abruptly.

Ryder turned and looked at her questioningly. Then he shrugged and walked a distance away. He turned his back to them and lit up a cigarette.

Chuck and Anna faced each other.

"I want to come with you," she told him.

His mind whirled. He took her hand and it was safely, wonderfully warm. "Anna, you can't," he said softly.

She paused a moment, and then she looked down. "I know. The things you've said, and Jerry said—the people who are after you are going to keep after you. I'd just slow you down. You'd always be worrying about me." He nodded and she continued, "And besides . . . I've made promises and commitments to Jerry. He really is a good man. A little dense sometimes, unwilling to listen. But I think that this trip has changed that. He's a better man for what happened, and I owe that to you."

He shrugged. "No charge."

Then he paused, clearly wanting to say something but not knowing the way to do it, or if he should. She sensed it immediately and said gently, "What's wrong?"

"Well . . ." He shrugged. "You agreed too quickly."

He sounded like a hurt puppy dog, and it couldn't help but make her smile. "What?"

"Well . . . when I said you couldn't come with me, it

would have been nice if you'd put up at least a *little* protest."

She laughed lightly in that wonderful way she had. "Just because I can't," she said, "doesn't mean that I wouldn't want to."

"Yeah. I guess so." He glanced in the direction of the fidgeting Ryder, who kept tossing surreptitious glances in their direction.

"Charlie," and she took him by the shoulders, "Look. I want to tell you something. I know what you've been going through. And I know what it must be doing to you. You're becoming both more brittle and more hardened. You're such a sweet, gentle man, and all these horrible, vicious things have been happening to you. Don't let it change you, Charlie. If it helps at all, always know that there is at least one woman who thinks that you're a wonderful human being, and the best part of herself."

She kissed him on the cheek and took a step back. And Chuck, arms folded, said, "Hey, Anna . . . if things were different . . . you think maybe . . . ?"

"If things were different, Charlie," she said with utter sincerity, "I never would have left you."

"Really?"

"Really. And I wish to God we could go back. But we can't. So all we can do is go forward."

"Yeah, but some of us have to keep watching our backs."

"We all do, Charlie. We all do."

She looked down at Rommel, who was glowering up at her. Then abruptly she kneeled down, took the muzzle of the surprised dog in her hands and kissed the top of his head, right on the "Z." Then she looked him square in the eyes and said, "You take good care of him."

Get your hands off me or I'll bite them off.

"He says he will," Chuck told her.

She talks took much. More than any human I've met. It's endless.

"And he says it was a pleasure meeting you."

She looked at him in wonder. "You really are in some kind of communication with him? You really understand what he thinks?"

"Oh, every word. You'd be amazed what he thinks."

"Well . . . " she sighed. "I knew you were a special man, Charles Simon. I just never dreamed how special."

At that point, unable to stand it any longer, Ryder stepped up and put a possessive arm around her shoulder. "Maybe you'd better get going," he said quickly. "You never know who could show up here who recognizes you."

"You're right, of course." He shook Ryder's hand and said "Thanks for those things you told me . . . about the government programs for mutations. That's valuable information. I'm not sure what I'll do with it . . . "

"At least you know," said Ryder. "Telekinetics is nice, but knowledge is the strongest power there is."

"Oh, absolutely." He looked significantly at Anna and said, "Sometimes the knowledge of certain facts is the only thing that keeps us going."

He inclined his head slightly and then turned and headed for an exit, Rommel following on his heels.

Very briefly, across the terminal, he caught a glimpse of Sandy Sendak. She was surrounded by reporters, who were interviewing her primarily because she was going to look really good on the evening news. She, in turn, spotted him, but she continued to politely talk to the reporters, making sure to show her good side, as her left eyelid descended in a quick wink.

He understood immediately. She was keeping her mouth shut about her personal knowledge of the man who had shared a cabin with her. Still, others would be more loose-lipped, and it was quite likely that certain people were going to realize just who was involved in the massacres aboard the Bullet Train, and just who had landed in New York City. He walked quickly, as if someone were right on his heels.

Where to now? Rommel asked him.

"Any preferences?"

And when Rommel spoke again inside his mind, it was with a melancholy very unlike the big dog's nature. *Yeah. Home.*

And just for the briefest moment, Chuck sensed an image of Anna in Rommel's mind.

"You and me both, fella," said Chuck wistfully, as they climbed the escalator out into evening-time Manhattan. "You and me both."